T0090421

SUN CHILD

A Meerkat's Tale

KRISTIN DOWNS

Order this book online at www.trafford.com
or email orders@trafford.com

Most Trafford titles are also available at major online book retailers.

Printed in the United States of America.

ISBN: 978-1-4269-4725-4 (sc)
ISBN: 978-1-4269-4726-1 (e)

Trafford rev. 11/30/2010

Trafford
PUBLISHING®   www.trafford.com

North America & international
toll-free: 1 888 232 4444 (USA & Canada)
phone: 250 383 6864 ♦ fax: 812 355 4082

A somber chill filled the air as the sun began to sink behind the Kalahari Desert. Many a meerkat clan had already bedded down for the night by this time, except for one. All was quiet at the golden-brown burrow entrance of the Isibani clan – usually there were nine, but on this particular evening, those sitting up outside the tunnel entrance were only seven. The dominant female, Isibani herself, was somewhere inside the burrow, as was her mate.

She, the queen of the clan, was dying.

All of the young adults and juveniles waited with bated breath in anxiety, until at last their father and leader emerged from the burrow. Though he tried to hide his heart-shattering sorrow from his children, some of them could see it in his eyes.

"Zarina," he murmured in a commanding voice.

Zarina, the "Golden One," stepped forward. She was the tallest and oldest of the youngsters, but not even she expected to be called forth. "...Yes, Father?" she chirped as she approached her Father.

"Your mother wishes to see you. Hurry now."

This was it, the moment Zarina had been dreading since the snake attack. Bravely, she took a deep breath and entered the burrow. Whatever her mother had to say, she knew fully well, it would be her last words.

Isibani's scent was still fresh in the faint air of the burrow tunnels, and Zarina followed the smell perfectly. She found her mother lying helplessly in between a hallway and a corridor, as if she tried in vain to reach a specific sleeping chamber. What stunned Zarina the most was the look of peace in her mother's face; she couldn't tell whether the wounded leader was asleep or had already passed on. But then, as Zarina crept closer, Isibani took a labored breath. She was still alive... but barely.

"Zarina..." her voice trembled weakly. "Zarina, my child. Is that you?"

"Its me, mother. I'm here." Zarina dared herself to move in closer to where she could see the open wounds left by the deadly snake on Isibani's right thigh. "Oh mother, your wound. It looks worse."

"Fret... Fret not, child," staggered the old leader.

"At least let me lick it clean."

"No... That won't be necessary," frowned Isibani. "My time is over, Zarina. I can feel it even now... I can hear the stars calling for me."

Zarina gasped in panic. "No mother! Please don't say that. You can't leave us, not now."

"Hush now, child." Isibani's voice was now reduced to a whisper, but it was enough to grab her daughter's attention. The old leader spoke slowly, but firmly:

"Listen, listen very closely, Zarina. There is a reason why I called for you... Of all my daughters, you have always been my most loyal, and my strongest warrior. There is no doubt in my heart... that you are the-the..." She struggled just this one time in her Final speech."...You are most worthy of my titles: Guardian, Mother, High Leader of the Clan."

"Mother, I... I don't know what to say."

"You needn't say anything child... Now, I have one last favor to ask you, Zarina."

"Anything," nodded the young leader.

"Tell the family... that I have passed on peacefully... that I've joined our ancestors in the sky... And, while I'm gone, take care of them. Especially the little ones; they'll be yours now."

"Yes, Mother."

"Promise me, Zarina... Promise me they'll be safe."
"I swear on my life that I'll take care of them, mother.
...Mother?"

Zarina nuzzled her mother's face gently, but it became clear that Isibani was beyond revival. She, the newly appointed leader, couldn't bear the thought of saying goodbye to one so noble and brave as her mother. After a few minutes of lying close to Isibani's body, Zarina pulled herself up on her feet. She would have to face her family with grave news, but as she slowly crawled out of the burrow, she could already feel newfound strength within herself.

"I will tell you, my little ones, of how we have all come to be:

"Many ages ago, the world was covered in eternal darkness. In those days, our ancestors had many more enemies than we do today. The hunters were all servants of the Dark, which gave them the edge over our poor ancestors. In fear for their lives, the first meerkats dug the first burrows; it was the only way they could avoid slaughter. While trapped in their caves, they prayed for days on end for a miracle. And then at last, He came: The Great Star!

"He, Nyota-Kuu, is the biggest and brightest of all stars. His light shone so brightly that it frightened most of the predators that dwelled in the Dark. They fled the desert, never to return. For the first time ever, our ancestors emerged from their burrows, no longer afraid of the Dark. And to this day, we owe our lives to the Great Nyota-Kuu, who brings us the light and warmth every day."

This was the gentle voice of Busara, lead female of the Kivuli clan. Whom she was telling the timeless Fable to were her latest offspring: three pups, one female and two male. It was important for them to know who Nyota-Kuu was, because now at three weeks old they were about to see the sun — as well as the world outside the burrow — for the very first time.

Standing proudly and anxiously outside of the burrow were the remaining members of the family, and standing taller than the rest was their father and leader: Shujaa. He was called such, because he was the toughest fighter his side of the Kalahari had ever seen - he was the "Champion."

Among his children, each close to adulthood, were "Jasiri the Bold," "Tani, the Powerful," "Jino, the Tooth," "Kucha, the Claw," "Jaraka the Swift," and "Makali, the Fierce." Shujaa named his children well, for each of them was expected to defend their territory from any invaders. Such was the way of the meerkat; defend or perish.

The Champion had already chosen names for his latest prodigy. The little female would be named Naima, which means, "Joy;" her mother Busara would appreciate a non-threatening name for at least one of her girls. One of the boys would be named after the Founding Father of the clan: "Kivuli, "the Shadow." The third one of the trio would be named "Madsada: the Supporter."

Still ushering the pups toward the burrow's entrance was "Busara, the Wise."

"Now," she murmured to her little ones, "Do not be afraid of the light, children. It may feel strange at first, but always remember: Nyota-Kuu is our friend. He would never bring harm to us... Are you three ready?" The pups chattered with excitement before their mother stepped outside.

It was all up to them now; the pups huddled together at the very edge of the burrow's entrance, until one of them was brave enough to meet the sun's rays at long last. That first brave one was Masada. He could hear the older members of his family cooing with excitement, but from Masada's point of view, they were standing on top of a mountain. It became clear that the only way that he and the other two pups could join the adults in the sun was to climb up a slope. It only looked hard; Masada was sure he could climb it.

As it turned out, the slope was much harder than Masada bargained for. The sand on the slope was as soft as silk; the pup couldn't even set his nails into it. He had to double-time his clawing until the sand began to slide and form a small step. But even the makeshift step couldn't help Masada up the slope; he needed an alternative. And that's when little Kivuli came trotting along. Just as he was finding his feet, the scheming Masada climbed onto his back in hopes to use him as a second step up the slope. The adults watching them chuckled, especially when it was little Naima who found the shortcut up the slope while the boys tussled.

Eventually, all three pups made it to the top and joined their extended family. The youngsters were all too willing to be groomed by their taller brothers and sisters, yet at the same time they were in awe at how huge and vast the earth was. But perhaps the strangest sight of all was the enormous ball of light in the sky. It was none other than the deity the pups were told about—the Great Star. Nyota-Kuu.

After everyone was well acquainted with the little ones, it was time for most of the family to go forage for food. The female, Tani, stayed behind to watch over the rambunctious pups.

"Who wants to play a game?" smiled Tani.

"Oh, I do! I do! Me!" cheered the pups.

"Alright," nodded the babysitter. "I'll close my eyes, and you three hide, then I'll come find you."

"You won't find me!" challenged Masada. "I already know the perfect hiding place."

Tani paid him no mind, and covered her eyes with her paws. "Okay, here I go. One... Two... Three..."

Kivuli and Naima scrambled in a frantic search for a hiding spot, which only boosted Masada's confidence in his cleverness.

"Ten! Ready or not, here I come!"

Tani was a clever meerkat in her own right; though the pups were already scattered and hiding, her keen sense of smell worked in her favor. In no time flat, she found Kivuli, snuggled behind a nearby rock, and Naima was found in a small patch of grass.

Masada, on the other hand, was slightly trickier to find. After ten minutes of sniffing around the area, Tani gave up.

"Alright, Masada, you win. Come on out now."

"Yay! I knew it! I knew you'd never find me!"

Masada knew that the entrance to the family burrow would have been the last place Tani would look for him.

After all, everyone saw how much he struggled to crawl over the slope between the surface and the tunnels.

He had his one brief moment of triumph, until Tani commanded, "Alright, Masada, good game. Now come on back up and join us."

That's when Masada's cleverness backfired; he only beat the slope once, and did so with help. Now he was all alone, facing the mountain again, and all his siblings joined in on was the laughter this time.

Later that evening, the whole family was together again, grooming and playing as the sun began to set, painting the sky with layers of blue, pink and purple. As the pups curled up to their mother, they watched in amazement as the sun seemed to sink into the earth.

"Mother!" Gasped little Naima; "The Great Star, it's going down!"

"It's gonna crash!" peeped Kivuli.

"Not to worry, my dears," Busara smiled wisely. "Nyota-Kuu is not only a friend to us, but he lives like us. You see, at the end of every day, The Great Star goes down into his own burrow, on the other side of the world."

"He has his own burrow?" asked Masada. "Where? How big is it?"

"No one knows," answered their mother, "but it's probably too far and too big for any of us."

"...Without the star," Frowned Naima, "the Dark will come back, won't it?"

"It's dark now," nodded Busara, "but it's nothing to worry about. No children, the Dark that terrorized our ancestors is gone for good."

"How do you know?" asked Naima.

Busara only needed to point straight upwards for the answer: "Look up there, my dears. Do you see those tiny little lights in the sky? Those are the spirits of all our relatives and ancestors who have gone before us. The Great One takes them to the sky when their time comes and together they light up the night, making sure no harm comes to our burrow while we sleep."

Naima pointed up at the full moon. "Which star is that, Mom?" "That," replied Busara, "is the first of all Night Stars. She is, perhaps, the first meerkat ever called to the sky. Her light is nowhere near as powerful as Nyota-Kuu's, but her presence is just as meaningful."

Masada thought for a moment, then asked, "Are we gonna join the night sky too, Mom?"

"Yes... someday- but hopefully not soon. I'd like to keep you little ones for myself for awhile." She giggled as she gave her babies a quick nuzzle.

Then without warning, the pups heard the unrecognizable sound of chattering. They soon realized that their father and older siblings were making the strangest clicking sounds.

"What are they doing Mom?" wondered Masada.

"They're singing," smiled Busara. "They're singing a lullaby for the Great Star. It's our way of thanking him for another peaceful day."

The youngsters were then finished with their questions. Their first day outside the burrow was both fast and eventful. As they listened more closely to the "lullaby," each one fell under the spell and drifted off into sleep. Soon the whole family would be sleeping underground, knowing they were being watched over and protected by a sky full of countless stars.

3.

One week after the tragic death of their leader, the Isibani clan was on the move to a new territory. Led by their father Gamba, the downtrodden clan marched into uncharted land full of uncertainty. And to make matters worse, gray clouds had overtaken the sky. Not even the sun could help them now.

Gamba came to a stop at a bare brush, and climbed all the way to the top of it to get a better view of the land. After a brief overlook of the barren wasteland, his attention turned to the sky.

"Looks like rain."

As Gamba descended from the tall bush, he could see the tired look in the eyes of his children. The clouds especially distressed the young female named Zola.

"We've got to find shelter," she alarmed. "There must be a bolt hole here somewhere!"

"There's still time to find a burrow," replied Gamba.

"Father," protested Zola, "if we don't find shelter of any kind soon, we may drown!"

"Patience, Zola! ...I can't lead the family anymore. This place is too strange, even for me." That's when the lead male turned to his eldest of daughters. "Zarina. This is your task."

Zarina, who was still struggling with her new power, was as stunned as her siblings. "Me, Father?"

Gamba gave here a sincere nod. "Only the clan's true leader can call upon the Great Star and ask for his help. You can do it, dear."

"But father--" said both Zarina and Zola at the same time.

"This is your chance to make your mother proud, Zarina. Call upon the Great One, and hurry!"

Zarina gulped; she had never even dreamed of talking to the Great Star in person; that honor belonged to Isibani alone. But as she looked and noticed her younger siblings shivering with cold and fear, she knew she had no other choice. This was the moment of truth. She slowly and carefully climbed up the bare brush that her father had, and glared at the sky. She had strong doubts at that moment that her voice couldn't even carry beyond the thick clouds. The young leader took a deep breath, and raised her paws to the sky in prayer.

"Oh Imbasa-Kulu, Great Star of the universe, hear me! I am Zarina, daughter of Isibani. My family needs your help, now more than ever. We need a new home — please show us the way! ...Please!"

There was an eerie whistle in the wind, but other than that, there was nothing. No sun, no light. Dismayed, Zarina descended the bush to rejoin her family.

No one seemed to notice it, but Zola shook her head with a small smile, as if she knew her sister couldn't pull it off. Zarina was no leader in Zola's eyes.

Zarina hung her head in shame; "I'm so sorry, Father. I tried... I--"

"Look!" yelled the juvenile female Abeni, as she pointed upward in amazement.

Everyone's heads followed Abeni's paw; sure enough, a cloud was moving. Even more amazing was the fact that small beams of sunlight shot through a gap in the clouds. Those sunrays were all pointing in one direction: North by Northwest. The whole family – aside from the speechless Zola – jumped and shouted with joy.

"You did it! You did it, Zarina! He answered us!"

Zarina was then showered with cuddles from her much younger siblings, while the older and wiser Gamba studied the direction in which the Great Star was "pointing."

"North by Northwest," he muttered. He then addressed the family: "Everyone! We know the way now, so let's follow it quickly! March!" They waited for Zarina to pass him; when she did, he cooed softly, "I knew you could do it, child."

The young female leader was still uneasy with her new power and only saw the occurrence as a stroke of luck. But the encouragement from her father made her smile. And so, the family was on their way... straight toward the heart of Kivuli territory.

4.

Gamba's intuition was correct; the rains came swiftly to the Kalahari that evening. Torrents of water drowned the barren desert, turning gorges into rivers, ditches into lakes, all in a matter of hours. No meerkat alive would dare brave the weather – they were all underground, whether in deep maze-like burrows or small emergency bolt holes. It would be another eight days before they would see their beloved sun deity again.

When the sun did reappear, most of the desert exploded into grassland. All trees and bushes that were bare one week earlier bore leaves and flowers. There were yellow buds littered all over the homeland of the Kivuli clan. For the pups, emerging from the burrow on that particular morning was like stepping into a new world – a green world, where creatures ruled both the earth and sky.

As for the pups themselves, they had gone through a change of their own; at nearly six weeks old, they were slightly bigger, more alert, and capable of foraging with the whole family. And foraging soon became their favorite activity; as soon as their father gave the word, they were gone in a flash.

Shujaa anticipated their charge, and was quick to catch up with them. With a voice like an army officer, he barked at the pups: "I'll not have you youngsters charging head first into the claws of a sky hunter!"

"What do you mean, dad?" frowned Masada as he slowed his gallop.

"Haven't I taught you little ones anything?" huffed Shujaa. "The hot season is teeming with predators. If you stray from us for a moment, they'll snatch you up and send you to the stars before you could even blink!"

"I thought going to the stars was a good thing," argued a puzzled Masada.

"It is a good thing," remarked Kivuli, "if you don't like living!"

Masada gave his brother a defiant huff and gave chase, only to be stopped by his father: "Masada! Know your place!" The boisterous pup then sat down in defeat.

Suddenly the air was cut through by a flock of small black birds. Naima saw them and panicked; "Sky hunters!" she shrieked as she hid between her Father's legs.

The wise Busara walked by; "Those are just drifters, Naima. The hunters are much bigger."

"Ha, ha!" teased Masada; "Naima's scared of tiny drifters!"

"Shut up," barked the female pup; "you were scared too – I saw you jump into that grass!" Naima was right, of course; Masada only hoped no one saw him hide from the swifts. His tail was still stuck between grass blades.

When the pups were done arguing, the group headed east to what they called "The Yellow Bed," which was a splendid patch of yellow flowers that seemed to go on for miles. It was the perfect nesting ground for insects and grubs – two of the meerkats' favorite meals.

To keep their energy up and their wits sharp, Tani, the older sister, challenged the pups to recite a poem they had learned earlier in the week. Each of the three pups took a verse, whichever one they knew best, but all together they chanted the first verse:

"Beware my pups, beware!

The world is a big and scary place,
And there you'll all be forced to face
The hunters and monsters who may give chase
To take your lives away
Beware of Horus, the king of the skies
Sharp are his talons, fierce are his eyes
He's sure to take you by surprise
If ever you dare to stray.

Beware, my pups, beware!

The Wadjet's legs were taken away
But still he hunts, night and day.
A single bite can take out his prey;
Beware his devilish hiss.
Beware Anubis, tall as a tree
Faster than wind on all fours is he
He's sneaky and clever, vicious and free
There's no greater hunter than this.

Beware my pups, beware!

Of all the dangers the land provides,
No matter who's stronger, no matter how wise,
There's no worse a threat to your demise
Than that of your own kind.

The rivals will chase you, they'll fight you, and still
They may even kill you if they so will
Perhaps for the land, the food, the thrill?
If ever you see them, hide!

If it's got claws, it's sure to scratch.
If its got teeth, it's sure to snatch.
If it's got talons, it's sure to catch.
They're sure to be everywhere,

So beware, my pups, beware!"

It was a clear afternoon in Yellow Bed Field. No beast or bird for miles would expect the phenomenon that was due to take place within the hour. As always, the youngsters Masada and Kivuli were more interested in chasing and wrestling each other than foraging. They knew there was plenty of food around thanks to the rains, so hunger wasn't the issue for them. Naima, on the other hand, was teaching herself how to dig as efficiently as her elders, and was learning fast. She was about to savor a tasty skink, when her littermates came tumbling by and tackled her, making her drop the wormy skink.

"What's the big idea, you two?" she growled.

"Sorry Naima," Kivuli apologized, who was in his feisty brother's chokehold.

"He started it," accused Masada, who was then pushed to the ground by his nimble brother.

At that moment, Masada laid flat on his back, and his big brown eyes were fixed on the gigantic ball of light in the sky. It was as if he was, for a very brief moment, hypnotized by it.

"Do you think Nyota-Kuu really does have a burrow?" he wondered out loud.

"Of course he does," nodded Naima. "Why else would he go underground every night?"

Masada sat up to look her in the eyes. "But he doesn't even look like a meerkat."

"Maybe he does," guessed Kivuli, "and he's just too bright to show his whole form."

"We'll never know for sure," said Masada, "...unless we go follow him to the edge of the world and find out."

Kivuli and Naima exchanged glances at one another before exploding into a fit of hysterical laughter.

"You're crazy!" said Naima.

"Stupid!" added Kivuli.

"No one has ever traveled that far from their home before."

"And those that tried got eaten by a hunter."

"Or slain by a rival clan."

Masada stood his ground. "You guys, just think what could happen if we did get that close to Nyota-Kuu. We could be heroes – no better, we'd be like legends!"

"Or," grinned Kivuli, "you could be punished for trespassing on his home turf."

"Yeah!" nodded Naima. "Remember the Wadjet? Nyota-Kuu took his legs from him for returning from the Realm of Darkness."

"You guys," argued Masada. "I ain't no enemy of The Great Star! When I get to his burrow, he may reward me! Maybe he'll give me wings, or a selket tail!"

"Or a kick in the butt," snickered Kivuli.

The youngsters meant him no harm, of course, they were just trying to stop their brother from making the biggest mistake of his life. But instead of discouraging Masada, they were only fanning the flames of his ambition. Masada then jumped onto his hid legs and announced, "I'm gonna do it!"

Kivuli and Naima gasped in horror, "Masada, don't!" warned Naima.

"Don't be an idiot," warned Kivuli harshly.

"I'm not an idiot!" growled Masada defiantly, "I will do it, and I'll come back a hero so big, they'll tell my story for ages to come!"

"Masada, no!" gasped Naima. But it was too late, he was gone in a flash, disappearing into a wall of tall green grass.

Already, Naima was panic-stricken. "Oh Kivuli, what'll we do?"

"Don't worry," replied her brother in a commanding voice. "You go back and tell mom and dad."

"But Masada?"

"I'll keep an eye on him," he assured her. "Now go!"

Naima tore through the flowerbeds in the opposite direction of Masada, while Kivuli gathered his thoughts and planned a strategy.

Far beyond Yellow Bed Field was a great hill of orange sand, and just beyond that was a gorgeous pasture of fresh green grass, with small trees and brushes scattered about. And taking advantage of this pasture was a herd of gemsbok—tall antelopes with striped backs and large black horns on their heads.

Standing atop the sand dune and taking it all in was the ambitious little Masada. He was so excited to be out on his own that he hardly even noticed the giant antelopes grazing below. It wasn't until he playfully slid down the dune and went tumbling into one of the gemsbok that he realized he was out of his element.

At first glance, he mistook it for a predator and scrambled behind the nearest tree. Then from his hiding place, he observed the huge creature as it used its lips to shovel up grass. Puzzled, Masada cocked his head.

"...Horn-heads eat grass?"

Masada kept staring at the grazer's quirky behavior, failing to notice that another gemsbok was trotting his way. But just as he fell into the shadow of a hoof, he was tackled and pushed to safety. Both dizzy and stunned, Masada took the push as an attack and raised his claws in defense. That's when he realized who pushed him:

"Kivuli!"

Kivuli was still trying to catch his breath after making a mad chase after his careless brother.

"Masada, you lucky dolt!" panted Kivuli. "That grass-eater was about to trample you!"

Masada was brushing off dust from his fur when he stated, "I saw him comin' a mile away... What're you doing here anyway?"

"I came to check on you."

"A-ha! So you too wanna see the Great Star's burrow!"

"That's not what I said."

"What, are you afraid? You wanna go cry home to Mama?"

"You're the one who's gonna cry when Mom spanks you for running away!"

"I don't cry as much as you, pup."

"You're a pup."

"You're a smaller pup!"

"No, you are."

"You are!"

A few shoves and spats were all it took to get the boys play-fighting again. In their tussle, both had forgotten about all other worries...but they were about to get a very, very big worry.

Hiding in tall golden grass, several feet from the pups and the gemsbok, was an old and injured jackal. In his desperation for food, he had picked up the faint scent of the meerkats. All he had to do now was bide his time and wait for the right moment to charge.

Slowly and steadily, the limp jackal crept through the thickets, but eventually he made a misstep, something the gemsbok picked up on immediately. The grazers let out a stark bellow, which alarmed gemsbok and meerkat alike.

The wily jackal, meanwhile, anticipated a stampede, so he laid low in the grass in hopes not to lose the element of surprise. His very survival depended on his one small meal.

Just as the jackal predicted, the alarmed gemsbok took flight and ran just past the deep thickets, just missing the jackal. The meerkat youngsters froze in terror as the ground shook and rumbled all around them. Still by the tree, they were safe from being run over by the gemsbok herd. But another problem ushered in: smoke rising in the wake of stampeding hooves, which made for a great cover for the old jackal. He crept in closer.

"Masada," coughed Kivuli, "we've got to get home!

Masada was also caught in the cloud of smoke. "How?" He sneezed; "We can't even see where we are!"

Kivuli followed his voice and crawled over to his brother.

"Here! Grab my tail," said Kivuli. "I'll lead us both outta here."

The trick worked well enough; the boys got as far as the thickets; Kivuli hoped he was crawling toward the orange dune, but instead went in the opposite direction. They were making it all too easy for the nearby jackal.

Just as they reached the forest of thick grass, the little ones' noses perked upward in curiosity.

"... You smell that?" whispered Kivuli worriedly.

"Yeah...What is it?"

"I dunno, but it smells like... like... death."

What Kivuli was about to find out was that he actually smelled the breath of a drooling, panting monster. The smoke cleared just as the starving jackal opened wide its jaws, as if inviting the pups inside. Kivuli saw long, yellow fangs and instantly screamed out:

"HUNTER!"

— SNAP! —

With lightning-quick reflexes, the pups leapt away as the jackal slammed it jaws shut.

"An Anubis!" gasped Masada. "Run!" He immediately turned to his right and took off. The 'Anubis' was about to make chase when he heard the squeal of another meerkat pup.

"Hey! Over here!" screamed Kivuli.

Kivuli turned to his left, knowing the beast would have to chose one pup over another. Initially, he chose Kivuli, forcing the brave young pup to dash into the sea of towering grass and brush.

Meanwhile, Masada ran straight around the grass and found a soft patch of sand that made his gait all the faster. He was instinctively heading for a bolt hole; lucky for him, an old abandoned burrow was waiting for him. It once belonged to a group of ground squirrels; perhaps the Anubis already got to them. Nevertheless, Masada had to reach it, or he'd meet with his end much sooner than expected.

In one final punch, he launched himself into the hole. Upon landing safely inside, he nearly inhaled dirt. But now that he had shelter, he could take a moment to breathe. And so he did.

But then he realized he was alone.

"Kivuli," he muttered, before taking a peek outside.

Kivuli had an advantage over the giant predator—something he never even imagined he would have. The old jackal walked with a tender foot, and the shade in the grasses made for good camouflage for the pup. He also weaved through the forest of grass in hopes to confuse his adversary. It worked well; with every ginger step, the jackal became more frustrated. Saliva was dripping from his mouth like raindrops. Soon his weary old heart could take the suspense no longer.

Masada kept a vigilant watch, knowing his brother was somewhere near. He was soon surprised to see him emerge from the thickets. And what was even more surprising was the shadow of the Anubis coming up right behind him.

"Kivuli!" screamed Masada. "Run! Run over here! Hurry, he's coming! Run Kivuli! He's right behind you!"

Kivuli followed Masada's voice, but once out in the open, he was a sitting target. He doubled his step and made a mad dash to the old burrow.

"That's it, run! Run faster! Hurry, Kivuli!"

The jackal made a desperate leap out of the thickets, but crash landed on his sore paw and let out a yelp in pain. This gave Kivuli his one and only chance to evade death. He galloped like a cheetah on steroids toward the burrow, while the Anubis found his feet and charged.

Masada couldn't turn his eyes away and even popped out of the burrow and stretched out his paws. "Come on! You're almost there! I'll catch you!"

Kivuli nearly lost his breath—and his vibrating heart—in his last stretch of the run. In his mind, Masada and the burrow looked like they were miles away. At one point, he could even feel the Anubis' rancid breath behind his head. Kivuli closed his eyes within the last two seconds and launched himself at Masada...

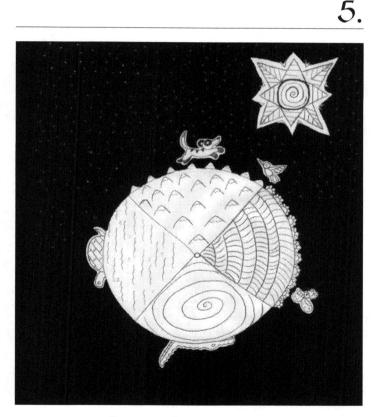

5

Humans call it a total solar eclipse. Meerkats would call it "The Return of the Dark." The strange and spooky phenomenon took place on the day that Masada and Kivuli disappeared, and it would be a day that would change the Kivuli clan forever.

Kivuli did indeed make the jump into Masada's arms, just as the old Anubis closed in on him. The two pups fell backward into the ground squirrel burrow, nearly knocking them senseless. It seemed to be all over for the Anubis, so the boys took a minute to slow their breaths to a more relaxed pace... But that would prove to be a costly mistake.

The jackal was standing just outside the burrow, intent on leaving only after snatching something. Anything. He started to dig.

The pups were only a few inches inside the burrow, and didn't think of moving further downward. And even if they did think of it, they were just too exhausted to move at all. That's when the earth rumbled again. This time, the soil all around them shifted; they thought for a moment that the tunnel was going to cave in on them. But instead, a shadow fell over the burrow entrance, and gigantic claws plowed into it. The boys were too terrified to even think at that point.

The next things Masada saw were teeth. The Anubis forced his muzzle inside the funnel entrance. The fangs desperately reached for the closest thing it could grab. In one moment, Masada had his brother in his arms. And in the next moment, Kivuli was gone.

Masada went into shock. He didn't know where he was, what it was, or even what day, week, month, or year it was. He just sat up in that burrow, jaw-dropped and eye-popped, staring silently at the now ravaged burrow entrance. When at last he recovered from shock, he slowly and cautiously climbed out of his hiding place. Part of him hoped against all hope that by some miracle, Kivuli was still alive, giving that old Anubis a bite on the nose.

What he saw instead was the adversary trotting away, looking far calmer and more satisfied than ever before.

As the jackal disappeared into the distance, the once blue sky was now fading to red. It wasn't evening, but Masada seemed to think it was, as he considered spending the night where he was.

The sky above him was going through a most bizarre change, but Masada would never notice. All he knew in that saddest of hours was that he was lost, exhausted, starving... and all alone.

Hundreds of meerkats paused from foraging that late afternoon and turned their attention to the color-turning sky. All were bedazzled at what they saw: a shadow creeping ever so slowly over their sun deity. The sun seemed helpless to stop itself from waning like the moon.

"What's happening?" they would whisper at first, until it became clear that as the sun started to disappear, so did the daylight.

"Oh my stars! The Great One is turning black!"

"It's the Dark. The Dark is returning!"

"The Dark is eating the star!"

When the eclipse became full, day seemed to warp into night and meerkat curiosity fell into outright panic.

"Run! Run to the burrow!"

"It's the end of the world!"

Only one family stayed outside that hour, while all others jumped into the closest bolt hole or home tunnel. That family, or course, was the Kivuli; after little Naima reported Masada running away, nothing — not even a sudden blackout — could stop their search.

Shujaa and his sons Jasiri and Makali had their work cut out for them as they tried to scan the skies and terrain for danger.

"I've never seen anything like this," muttered Shujaa.

"It's like nighttime came early," agreed Jasiri.

"It must be an omen," said Makali.

The nearby Busara overheard them and growled, "I don't care what it is! We must find Masada and Kivuli before it's too late! Move onward!"

"Mother," panicked Tani, "I can't see a thing."

"Use your nose, everyone. We can still smell," advised Busara. "No darkness is going to keep me from my babies."

With twice the determination as the others, Busara bravely pushed forward, through tall grass and thick brush until she came upon the huge sand dunes that stood before the gemsbok-grazing field.

Descending from the dune proved difficult; Shujaa and Busara both slid down like professional snow-boarders, while their children tumbled like rocks. But they were close now — Busara felt it in her bones and smelled it in her nose.

"I can smell them... They're near! Masada!! Kivuli!! Mommy's here!"

Her calls would fall on deaf ears. Masada was within a mile from his family by this time, but he had already lost his brother and had fainted from exhaustion.

Busara kept up her search, inching closer and closer to the lake of thickets and tall grass — the only thing standing between her family and Masada. But navigating through this terrain proved to be most difficult. With no sunlight, the clan kept bumping into things, and each other. Worse yet, they picked up a most disturbing smell.

"...Anubis," muttered Shujaa gravely.

"No," gasped Busara in horror. "...No, I can still smell them. They're alive, I know it!"

"Busara," frowned her doubtful mate.

"Come on, Shujaa! Follow me!"

Elsewhere, the younger meerkats were having trouble:

"Ouch! Who just stepped on my tail!?"

"Sorry, Tani, that was me."

"Makali?"

"Yes."

"Where are you?"

"I'm here!"

"Where?"

"Here! Grab my tail! ...There you go, Tani."

"I'm Haraka," replied the one holding Makali's tail.

"Jasiri? Is that you?"

"Over here, Jino!"

"...Ouch!" they both peeped, bumping heads together.

The others collided with the branches; Haraka was particularly injured with a bloodied hind leg. But still they pressed on.

In just a few more minutes, the earth's shadow began to release the sun, and light returned to the desert. The young adults cheered jubilantly, but Busara remained focused on finding her missing pups. Once her vision was clear, she found herself on the edge of the grass field, and charged through. She then let out her lead calls to the group: "Everyone! Over here!"

One by one, the Kivuli clan emerged into the light, weary, but relieved. Shujaa could now see paw prints in the sand; some belonged to his sons, others belonged to a terrible danger. "They were here," confirmed the leader; "...they were chased by the Anubis... They stopped here."

He and Busara stood outside the ground squirrel burrow, which now looked like it was completely dug up. Their hearts sank with grief; surely the beast caught them here, and ate them.

As the rest of the family gathered around the scene, they each quietly came to terms with the fate of their youngest of kin. Even little Naima was present, and was just as heartbroken.

Shujaa inched himself over to his devastated mate, in an attempt to comfort her. "Busara?" She shook her head in despair. "Dearest..." Shujaa tried to put his paw on her shoulder, but she shook it off.

"No!" she cried out. "My babies... My poor, poor babies..." Not being able to say another word, Busara sobbed as she led the charge back home.

Later that evening, they would all hold a ceremonial gathering at their burrow. It would be the last time for a long time Busara would look directly into the sun. As far as she was concerned, Nyota-Kuu had betrayed them. His eclipse doomed her pups, a double-blow to the heart of a devoted mother. Busara made a silent promise to herself that night, that she would never speak to her sun god again.

As Masada slept through most of the eclipse, he fell into the strangest dream. He saw a meerkat — at least it looked like a meerkat given its simplistic appearance. It might have even been Masada himself.

He, the meerkat, was running across a land full of high hills, even mountains. His head was raised to stare intently at what appeared to be Nyota-Kuu as he floated across the sky.

The meerkat only stopped to speak to a small bird.

"Where are you going?" she asked him.

"I'm following the Great Star," replied the meerkat. "I'm going to catch him!"

"He's too far away," said the bird. "You can't run that far."

"I'll show you," argued the meerkat. He then ran so far that he left the hills and came across a vast green meadow.

In the meadow, he came across a small butterfly.

"Where are you going?" she asked him.

"I'm following the Great Star," he replied. "I'm going to catch him!"

"He's too fast," said the butterfly. "You'll never out-run him."

"I'll show you," replied the defiant meerkat, and took off faster than ever before.

Soon the meadow became a big blue lake, and in the middle of it was a crocodile. The reptile floated over to the beached meerkat.

"Where are you going?" smiled the crocodile.

"I'm following the Great Star," replied the meerkat. "I'm going to catch him!"

"He's too high up," said the reptile. "You can't jump that high."

"I'll show you," replied the defiant meerkat. He then jumped right on top of the crocodile and lunged himself clean over the lake, landing safely on the other side. Again, he took off after the sun.

Eventually, the little meerkat ran into a land that was flat and rock-hard. He only stopped when he came across a large tortoise.

"Where are you going?" asked the tortoise.

"I'm following the Great Star," answered the meerkat. "I'm going to catch it!"

"...And why would you do that?" asked the tortoise. "Are you going to keep him all to yourself?"

For once, the meerkat was stunned. "I... I don't know. I guess we'll find out when I catch him."

"Ha!" laughed the tortoise. "The great Star doesn't belong to just anybody, but everybody. That's why you won't catch him."

"I'll show you!" huffed the meerkat, and took off after the sun once again.

What the meerkat didn't know was that the tortoise was right: No one could catch the Great Star. And no matter how far he could run, the meerkat would always be right behind the sun; for the world, as it turns out, is circular and therefore the sun stays in the air. The meerkat, however, would keep running around the world, passing the same hills, same meadow, same lake and same wasteland, forever and ever, too stubborn to listen to reason.

It was, indeed, a strange dream, but one which gave Masada a little enlightenment. But as he slept on, he had no idea that his family was leaving him behind. He would soon wake up to a nightmare, full of unexpected – and deadly – surprises.

6

Shortly after the great blackout came to an end, the Isibani clan rose from the bolt holes they were hiding in. First to greet the sun was the head of the family, Gamba, followed by Zarina his daughter. Appearing out of a different bolt hole were Zola, along with identical twin brothers Anguka and Choma ("Crash" and "Burn" respectively).

Ushomi, the eldest of Gamba's sons, stayed closest to the three smallest of his sisters: Abeni, Imbali, and Tamu. The juveniles were not much older than Masada, at just four weeks old. This was to be their first time foraging independently with their elders, and it turned out to be a complete disaster.

Abeni clung onto Ushomi's leg and trembled with fear; "Is it over?" she whimpered.

Ushomi bent down to nuzzle her head. "It's okay, look. Imbasa-Kulu is back and brighter than ever!"

"But what if the Dark comes back?" asked the frightened pup.

That's when Gamba came over to check on his little ones and overheard them peeping with fear. "Fear not, my girls," he purred. "Imbasa-Kulu has defeated the Dark, and always will. Tonight we will sing his praises like never before."

Zola, the second-oldest female, crawled over to Zarina with a look of worry in her eyes. "Of all days for the Dark to return, why today? Does the universe know something we don't?"

"What do you mean, Zola?" asked the clan leader.

"Mother Mweza, the Great Moon, wanes and disappears at times, but never Imbasa-Kulu. This was more than some comeback by the Dark; The Great One might be trying to tell us something."

"You think it was a sign?"

Zola nodded solemnly. "I believe something terrible is going to happen to us, and He knows it."

Zarina felt a chill. Her sister was always a superstitious one, even for meerkat standards. But when she felt a bad omen, she was usually right. For once, since Zarina's crowning, Zola was on her side. "If something is to happen to us," said Zarina, "we'll face it together as we always do."

"Just keep your eyes and ears open, sister. We're all depending on you now; don't screw it up."

Zarina took Zola's words to heart; there may have been tension between them, but when it came down to it, both girls put the family first. In her heart, Zarina prayed that she would never "screw it up."

Suddenly, Gamba appeared before them with his tail raised in alert. "Stay sharp, girls! Ushomi and I have picked up a predator's scent."

Zola jumped on all fours and raised her own tail; "What is it, Father? Anubis? Wadjet?"

"Follow me," was all he said before leading the way.

Zarina gulped worriedly; was this the danger Zola warned her about?

When at last Masada gained consciousness, he felt ten years older. Still reeling from the Anubis attack, he struggled to pull himself out of the burrow he took shelter in. His stomach ached with hunger, but his top priority was finding his way home. The problem with that was he completely forgot the way, so he began to wander aimlessly, calling out as loudly as he could.

"Mom... Dad... Jasiri? Tani? Makali? Naima? ...Anybody? ...Mom?! Dad?! It's me, Masada! Where are you?"

For every other creature that may have heard his cries they only came out as high-pitched squeaks: "Brr! Brr! Brr! Brr!"

For a hungry predator, it would have been music to their ears. But the only predator in the area would not hear those cries, for it was totally deaf. But it would have its chance to nab Masada anyway.

Masada, feeling his legs grow heavy, made the mistake of stopping in the middle of a grass patch to rest. He leaned back on what he thought was cold and perfectly round tree branch. What it turned out to be was the coiled body of a cape cobra. It too was resting, but at the moment it felt Masada's presence, it reared its yellow head in curiosity. Soon enough, it flicked its forked tongue toward the pup, which to Masada felt almost like a lick. Panic struck immediately. He jumped onto his four paws and all at once his strength came back to him. The pup ran straight into tall grass and thickets, with the "Wadjet" close behind.

Masada ran in a direction he never had before; he was moving further and further away from home. But with a hungry monster slithering close behind, he didn't have time to think about the family.

There was another problem: without knowing his way, Masada never would have guessed that he was headed straight for a steep sandy slope. Plus, he seemed too interested in seeing how close behind the Wadjet was. As it turned out, it was quite nimble for a creature with no legs.

And then as fate would have it, he slipped and tumbled down the hill, nearly knocking himself unconscious upon landing on flat ground.

The yellow cobra gracefully zigzagged downward toward its bewildered prey. Masada only had a few seconds to climb back up on his feet and resume running. But as he ran, he was clearly losing energy. Only one thing kept the Wadjet from this small meal, and that was a thorn bush. Masada used the last ounce of strength he had to reach the shady plant and cling onto its lowest branches.

Seeing that it now had to brave a branch of thorns, the cobra looked defeated. However, it stuck around just to see if there were any small openings under the bush for a calculated strike. But it would never get that chance.

Masada quietly said his prayers to the stars for a miracle, and then all of a sudden the Wadjet stopped its stalk. In fact, for a moment, it was frozen stiff. It sensed the presence of enemies – many of them. It pulled itself back, away from the thorn bush, as if terrified.

Then Masada heard something the Wadjet could not. Growl calls... Meerkat growl calls! He gasped in amazement, realizing a clan was nearby. In his position, he couldn't care less as to who was coming to his rescue, so long as they were!

The truth of the matter was the Isibani clan had no idea there was a helpless pup hiding beneath the thorn bush nearby. All they knew for certain was that there was a deadly Wadjet in their foraging area, and they wanted it gone!

Led by Gamba, the whole family formed a line and carefully made a half-circle around the snake. They growled like fierce lions and spat like furious llamas in front of the predator. It couldn't hear their calls, but it could feel their aggression. Only when a single meerkat broke ranks did the Wadjet attempt to strike, but his enemies were too quick for him. The cobra would try three more times to launch a venomous bite, but Isibani raged on and forced the snake into a corner.

Seeing no other way out except to retreat, the humbled Wadjet exited into a forest of tall grass. After making sure he was gone, the Isibani quickly transformed from a fearsome mob to a jubilant team.

"Get back to the pits, you legless freak!"

"Yeah, you tell 'em bro!" cheered the twins Anguka and Choma. "We sure showed that sand-crawler, didn't we?"

"Yeah. Nobody messes with the Isibani!"

Still hiding in the thorn bush's shade was Masada. He sat in silence, awestruck by the strangers, and wasn't sure of whether to feel scared or grateful by their presence. He decided not to risk more danger and stay quiet – if they didn't see him, he would most certainly be safe.

The Isibani were about to move on, when their High Leader Zarina noticed a strange figure in the shadows. When she moved in for a closer look, she noticed it had eyes. Before anyone else took notice, the bright-tan female crawled over the thorn bush, where her instincts were confirmed: a meerkat pup was hiding there!

Masada was trembling; he learned from his elders that strangers were dangerous. He knew for sure that this one facing him would attack him mercilessly.

Zarina's eyes softened, and her heart melted. A baby. And it was all alone – an orphan, perhaps. The very sight of the strange pup made here realize something: She truly was her mother's daughter, and all she needed now was a child of her own.

"Aww," she cooed. "Where'd you come from, little one?"

Masada couldn't speak. He could only shake.

"Don't be afraid," shook Zarina's head. "I'm not gonna hurt you. Come here..." She softly reached out to him.

Gamba was the first to notice that Zarina had wandered off elsewhere. When he saw her crouching down by a thorn bush, he quickly became concerned. "Zarina! ...Zarina, what are you doing over there?" Imagine his shock when his eldest daughter turned to face him while holding a strange pup in her arms. He rushed to her side, eyes beaming in alarm. "Zarina... what is that?"

She smiled calmly at him. "It's a pup, Father. I think he was hiding from the Wadjet."

It didn't take long for Zarina's family to gather around the scene. They were all as shocked as their Father.

"That's not one of ours," frowned Zola.

"It doesn't matter," said Zarina sternly. "He needs our help."

"No, Zarina," her Father replied coldly.

"...But Father-"

"You know the law! Strangers are not allowed into our family without complete consent of the leaders. And I say no to this one."

"He's just a pup, Father!" What harm can he do?"

"Plenty!" shouted Zola nearby. Suddenly all eyes were on Zarina's outspoken littermate. "Did I not tell you about the omen? The Great Star cast his shadow over us as a warning! He knew we'd find this stranger and he would bring a curse upon our home if we take him in! We must get rid of it!"

"Zola!" roared Zarina. "How could you say such things about a child?!"

"Father doesn't trust him, and neither should we."

Zarina bared her teeth at Zola. But then, Gamba spoke up: "I'm afraid Zola's right, Zarina. We can't take this pup in; his clan may be nearby."

"That too bodes ill for us," added Zola.

"And even if he is all alone," Gamba continued, "There is no proof, no historical evidence that a pup from outside our clan could ever truly fit in."

"He could very well turn on us," nodded Zola.

"Enough!" cried out Zarina as she clung onto little Masada. Gamba's tone softened, but his attitude remained cold. "I am sorry Zarina, but my decision remains final. Either we leave that stranger where it is... or we kill it."

Zarina felt powerless, as her father seemed to take complete control of the situation. Not one to disobey her father, she bowed her head in defeat.

"Anguka. Choma." Gamba called the twins forward to carry out the execution; clearly his mind was made up.

Meanwhile, a sympathetic Zola nudged Zarina away from the scene, whispering to her, "You don't have to watch, sister."

Masada was left sitting all alone, facing two older male meerkats with bared teeth, stalking him intently. The pup desperately cried out for help by barking as any distressed pup would. Only Zarina responded to the barks by turning to spy on the grim scene. Her brothers decided to attack from two sides, to block the pup from escaping. As they closed in on the crying pup, Zarina's tolerance level finally reached its limit. When they came down on Masada, she made her move.

"NO!"

Anguka and Choma jumped back as their big sister jumped into the fray and shielded Masada with her body. The family paused in surprise, while the terrified pup received gentle cuddles and purrs from her savior.

A furious Gamba marched toward her. "Zarina! How dare you diso--"

"Listen, Father! I am the High Leader of this family. Only I can decide who lives or dies! And I say this pup deserves a chance to live with us!"

Gamba was taken aback; never did he expect Zarina to act so defiantly, or speak so demandingly. Even if she was

High Leader, she never showed it until this moment. Not knowing how to respond to this new Zarina, he let her speak her peace.

"Mother believed in me. She said I had it in me to be a great leader, and a great mother. This could be my only chance to honor her. Let me raise this child, Father; I can teach him our ways, and I'm sure he'll make us all proud... Please, Father... Please."

Gamba needed a moment to let his emotions settle down. Then realized his daughter was right. Isibani did choose her, and her choices were never wrong. Finally, he took a deep sigh. "Don't make me regret this."

She gave him a gentle and relieved smile.

"Let's go home," commanded Gamba.

The others followed suit with Zarina carefully holding her new pup by the scruff of his neck in her mouth. No one, not even Zola, would give her or Masada a hard time again- at least, not for the remainder of that day.

The evening proved to be peaceful for the Isibani. But even though most of the clan had accepted him by then, Masada still felt like an outsider. He was even too shy to speak. This didn't concern Zarina; she knew how to bond with pups. She invited the quiet one to sit by her and her littlest of sisters to watch the sunset, while the rest of the family sang their praises to Imbasa-Kulu.

That was one thing that bothered Masada. Why did they call The Great Star "Imbasa-Kulu?" Wasn't His name "Nyota-Kuu?" What did this mean, he wondered?

"Look, girls. Look up there," said Zarina as she pointed to the evening's brightest of stars. "There's our mother, Isibani. She's watching over us from way up there."

"Wow," cooed little Abeni. "She's so beautiful."

"Yes," Zarina said solemnly. "Yes, she always was beautiful."

"I miss her," frowned Imbali.

"I know. I miss her too," replied Zarina. "But we will be with her again some day.""

She then turned to the quiet one. "Do you have anyone up there, little one?"

Masada reared his head up to the star-filled sky, and in remembering his brave brother Kivuli, he nodded sadly.

Zarina inched closer to him. "We all lose something precious to us as we get older. It's one of life's ultimate tests. It may hurt you — it may even make you question yourself and why you're here. I know how that feels. Everyday, I ask myself why my mother chose me to lead this family. I also wonder if I can be as good a leader as she was... You see, children, we're never sure what's going to happen tomorrow. All we can do is hope for the best and stay together as a team. As a family."

Again she looked to the quiet one, who seemed to be listening to her curiously. "You've nothing to fear from us anymore, child. You're a part of this family now. It might take them time, but soon they'll all love you, as I love you."

Masada gave a soft sigh. For the first time since the eclipse, he felt safe. In fact, he now felt safe enough to speak: "Masada."

"Hmm?" purred Zarina. "What'd you say?"

"My name... It's Masada."

"Masada. That's a beautiful name. I'm Zarina."

"Zarina."

"Yes... It's very nice to meet you."

They exchanged smiles, and watched the rest of the sunset side by side.

7

Masada would prove his merit to the Isibani soon
enough. On the next day, when the family went foraging,
he went along with them with a newfound spirit. He was

now close to six weeks of age, old enough to catch his own food. He was looking forward to it.

The foraging party settled in a green pasture surrounded by trees as tall as baby giraffes; they called it, "Tree Valley." Most of the group found interest in a giant fallen tree branch, where thousands of tiny grubs crawled underneath. For young Masada, the best part of the branch was the top of it; he took pleasure pouncing on Ushomi and Zarina while their heads were to the ground. None of the others seemed interested in playing, not even the usually feisty twins Anguka and Choma. When the pup asked them about finding or sharing food, they gave him the cold shoulder. He needed a new strategy.

He wasn't about to sit up and beg, like the four week-olds. Yet their begging actually worked!

"Okay kids, who wants this one?" Ushomi or someone else would ask while holding up a grub.

"Oh! Oh! Me! Me! Me! ME!!" the littlest girls would cry out. The loudest cries would win the snack. Masada was above that. It was time to dig.

After a fruitless fifteen minutes of constant shoveling, Masada turned to an abandoned ditch already carved out by Zola. This hole in the ground proved to be a gold mine, with a long pink skink lodged inside it. But just as he had pulled it to the surface, little Tama came out of nowhere and grabbed the other end of it. The two youngsters broke out into a tug of war, which ended with the skink breaking in two, sending pups flying.

Masada somersaulted backward, right into Zola. Her head, which was already buried in dirt, was pushed in further painfully.

"Ow! What the... you," she growled. To compensate for her headache Masada quickly handed over his half of the skink and scuttled off.

Feeling defeated and hungry, Masada turned to his new mom Zarina. She was already waiting for him with good news: "Masada, come over here! Look..."

Masada could not believe his eyes as he followed Zarina to an isolated patch of grass. Hiding inside it was a small creature with six legs, two huge claws, a curved prickly tail and a black exoskeleton. He had heard of this creature before, but until now had never seen one. He cheered with excitement, "A Selket! A real-life Selket!"

"And it's all yours," smiled his guardian.

Despite the scorpion's violent appearance, Masada was at the winning end, and he knew it. The pup couldn't help but dance around his would-be meal like a child in a candy store. He didn't expect it to fight back, but that's just what it did! As soon as the pup's nose was in range, it pinched him fiercely.

"Ouch!"

"That's strike one!" cheered the nearby Choma- or was it Anguka? Whoever it was, his twin brother laughed in agreement.

Very soon the rest of the clan gathered around, curious to see just how long the fight between newcomer Masada and the Selket would last.

"Come on pup, give 'im hell! Chew it up n' spit it out!" shouted the other twin.

Now with fire in his eyes, Masada cautiously circled the scorpion, avoiding the black pincers.

"Go for the tail! The tail!" cheered Ushomi.

"He's too young; let me handle it," suggested Zola.

"No," insisted Zarina, "give him a chance, he can do it."

"By stars, it looks good!" cooed Imbali. "Can we split it?"

Just after she said that, Masada took a quick bite at it, but was immediately met with the scorpion's stinger. It got him right on the forehead, but its venom would never affect him. All he felt was the painful pinch, and it made him all the more determined. He bit at the tail this time, and got pinched by a scissor-shaped pincer.

"Strike two!"

"Strike three!"

"And he's still in the game!"

"Choma! Anguka, quiet!" barked Zarina.

"But we're keeping score," replied one of the twins.

"He's going to lose an eye," worried Zola.

"Come on, Masada, bite the tail!" cheered his guardian.

"Yeah," smiled a twin, "like this!" as he bit into his brother's.

"Yow!" screamed the other twin. "What was that for!?"

"Sorry bro, I just--"

"I'll make you sorry!" They tackled each other.

The duel between Masada and the Selket went on another minute, and then the pup took a few more pinches from his opponent. So many, in fact, that the audience started to cringe in empathetic pain. "Ooo... Ow... Augh!"

"That's not right!" reacted Ushomi, holding his underbelly.

Then, at last — **CHOMP!** — The duel ended abruptly, with Masada victoriously severing the Selket's middle.

"Yay!" cheered Zarina. "Let's hear it for the new Selket Wrestling Champion!"

"Hooray! Yay Masada!" they all cheered. "Way to go! Hooray Masada! Masada! Masada!"

"Intruders!!" called out Gamba suddenly.

All at once, the mood turned from delightful to fearful. Everyone stood on their toes in the direction Gamba was facing. They saw shadows creeping in the distance; the enemies' faces hidden by grass. But it was clear that they were meerkats; their raised tails proved it.

"My stars. Rivals," gasped Zarina in horror.

"Let's hope they don't see us," gulped Zola.

"Too late!" barked Gamba. "They're coming!" From his sentry post on the tree log, he could see the rivals jumping and leg-kicking in the traditional war dance manner, straight into their direction.

Zola bravely stepped forward. "Come on, we can take them! Forward!" She then mimicked the rivals by kicking her back legs in the air.

"No! Stop!" called out Zarina.

"What!?" gasped her sister in surprise.

"Just wait," demanded the High Leader.

Zarina then took to her Father's side to get a better view of the opposition. One by one, she counted them.

"Two... Four... Eight? ...My stars. Too many!"

"Zarina!" called out Zola. "Do we fight or not?"

Zarina's heart ran a marathon, looking back to her young charges and to the charging army again. She had only one solution: "Retreat... Retreat!"

"Retreat!" echoed Gamba. "Fall back to the burrow!"

The family was horrified, but they had no choice but to obey. To signal the retreat, they first took a few quick paces backwards, and then ran in the opposite direction of the oppressors. They disappeared into the tall grass, where the rivals would lose sight and scent of them.

Victory was in sight for the Kivuli clan. Once they saw off the strangers, they cheered in delight and began to mark their scent all over the tree log.

Jasiri took to his father's side and patted his back.

"Well done, Father! We showed those trespassers, didn't we?"

"Hm," growled the unpleasant Shujaa. "First, I lose two sons, and now I stand to lose my home!?"

He then addressed the whole clan: "Hear me, my children! We may have won this day, but this is only the beginning. If these strangers want to stay, then this is war! We must be willing to do whatever it takes! Are you with me, my children?"

"Hurrah!" they cheered in reply.

"Then," said the leader, "let them all hear our name!"

"Kivuli! Kivuli! Kivuli!"

Meanwhile, the Isibani returned home with a bitter defeat under their belts. "Imbasa-Kulu betrayed us," mourned Abeni.

"Now-now," consoled her father. "He cannot choose one clan over another. That's not his way."

Zola then approached her other leader very bitterly: "We should have war-danced. Our numbers might have frightened them away."

"We couldn't risk it," argued Zarina. "We have pups to think about." Then another thought crossed her already troubled mind: "Maybe I was wrong to lead us here. Maybe we should move on."

"Don't even think it," growled Zola. "We risked a lot to get here, we can't just give it all up. We should fight for this place."

"What if mother were still here? Would you listen to her?"

"Mother wouldn't have run away!"

"Enough!" barked Gamba. "...Zola has a point, Zarina. We don't have to leave, not just yet. There's still hope... But you, Zola; you must listen to your sister. She's never steered us wrong before." Zola bowed her head in submission.

"And that's the end of it," sighed Gamba. "Let's all get some rest. We'll decide what to do about the rivals soon enough." He then left the two eldest daughters alone for a moment.

But in that moment, Zola softly spoke her peace to Zarina: "Nobody wants a coward for a leader." She then sank into the burrow for a rest.

Zarina kept a vigilant watch with her brother Ushomi up until sunset. All was peaceful in their home turf for the remainder of that day, but Zarina now began to wonder how much longer that peace would last... and also wondered if her sister Zola had a point about her leadership.

8

After traveling many miles, risking life and death, the Isibani clan's last agenda on earth was getting caught up in war. But after realizing they've stumbled upon another clan's land, that's just what they got. And everyone knows that where there's war, there are bound to be casualties. Not willing to risk it, they had decided to stay as close to their burrow as possible, while a select few went out in search of a new one. The pups, including young Masada, were forbidden to leave the premises until it was safe. But eventually, even meerkats get cabin fever.

"Come on, Ushomi, show us the tree-eaters!" begged the little ones that afternoon. "You promised us."

Their caregiver that day was the eldest of Gamba's sons. He had promised to take the pups out further than normal, but that was before the encounter with the Kivuli. "I told you pups," said Ushomi, "We can only go as far as Thorn Bush; the tree-eaters live all the way out in Wetland."

"Pleeeeease?"

"We'll only take two minutes!"

"Yeah, the others'll be back by then."

"Maybe even later!"

Ushomi sighed.

"Just show us one tree-eater," begged Masada. "One's all we need to see."

"Yeah!" squeaked his new sisters.

"Well..."

"Can they really eat a whole tree?" wondered Abeni.

"Well no," explained their big brother, "but they can reach the tallest branches."

"Could they eat the clouds too?" smiled Masada excitedly.

"I don't know if they're that tall."

"But definitely taller than Anubis?"

"Definitely taller."

"Well, what're we waiting for?" peeped Imbali. "Let's go!"

"Hold it! Wetland is very, very wet. You'll get your coats soggy, and I know you pups don't like that."

"So?" argued Masada. "It'll be worth it!"

"Yeah!" cheered the girls in unison.

51

Ushomi was at a loss. "Okay. One tree-eater, two minutes."

"Yay!!" was the unanimous response.

The Kivuli awoke to a bittersweet morning. Busara the Matriarch was in the first happy mood in days, since the heart-breaking loss of her youngest sons. But now she had a reason to be hopeful: she was pregnant. She smiled warmly to her mate that morning while sitting in the sun. "The stars have been merciful to us, my love."

"Hm?" he purred curiously.

"I can feel changes in me. I can tell it's a sign of our next litter."

"Ah!" he smiled excitedly. "So the Great One has answered our prayers then."

"Your prayers, perhaps..." she sighed.

"Busara, don't tell me you still blame Nyota-Kuu for what happened two days past."

"If He hadn't cast his shadow on us, we would have our boys."

Shujaa frowned grimly. "We would have seen them being devoured by the Anubis. I'm sorry, dearest, but I believe the Great One saved us that day. He spared us from a horror that would give us nightmares for years to come."

"Maybe you're right," she murmured. "But I still feel wronged by it..."

"Don't worry, Busara dear. Kivuli and Masada are in a better place now. And once we rid ourselves of those strangers, our next brood will have that much better a start in life."

"That's the other thing that troubles me," said the matriarch. "Must we go to war with them? Wouldn't it be easier to just head out west and look for new pasture?"

Shujaa could only laugh; "Hahahaha! Didn't you see how terrified they were yesterday? One more charge and I can assure you they'll run straight to the edge of the earth!"

Busara was not so confident; "They have pups of their own, love. They'll defend them to the death if it comes to that. And I must say, Shujaa, I am not willing to let it come to that."

Shufaa took a moment to watch his children frolic around the burrow. He observed little Naima most intently. "Look at her," he said, "She's barely a month old, and already she's keeping up with Tani and Haraka. It won't be long now until she's fit to defend this land alongside us."

"She shouldn't have to," frowned Busara. "She's all that's left of our last litter, poor child. I bet she thinks of her brothers at every second."

"She's got a strong will, just like her mother," assured her mate. "When the time comes, we'll appoint her as top babysitter of the new litter."

"Yes," Busara nodded in agreement. "I think she'd like to be around young ones again."

"I'll go back to what you've said earlier," said Shujaa, "about not wanting to risk more loss. I agree with you there, my love, but let us test them. I will take Jasiri, Makali, Tani, and Haraka to wherever those strangers are hiding. If we manage to flush them out and give chase, then we can be certain they'll not bother us."

"It would be better if we split up," replied Busara. "I'll take the girls, and you take the boys."

"So you're up to it are you?"

"I am... but I hope you're right about them being cowards. I hope they run away this time, and for good."

They settled on their decision with a gentle nuzzle.

By late afternoon, Ushomi and his charges were already nearing Wetland, which was a patch of soft earth where a small river could be, depending on how much rainfall there would be at any given time. Grass was never greener, nor trees taller than in this humble little field. Ushomi kept the little ones entertained by telling them silly stories during the long journey:

"And then," he spoke with a false growl in his breath, "just as the fearsome reptile crawled closer and closer to his prey, that's when the sky let out a mighty roar!! It was Imbasa-Kulu, and He said to the Wadjet, 'How dare you crawl back here from the Dark! I'll punish you for this!' And then, He threw down a piece of his own hand, and when it fell onto the Wadjet, it crackled loudly."

"You mean like thunder?" asked Masada.

"It was thunder!" exclaimed Ushomi. "It was the first thunderbolt anyone had ever seen, and the Great Star still uses His thunderous hands to keep away all the Dark's children."

"What does thunder sound like?" asked Imbali.

"Like this: KABOOM!" jumped Ushomi.

"Waah!" the girls wailed; startled, they scattered and hid behind grass patches.

Now that he had the all-knowing Ushomi alone, Masada was poised for some more questioning. "My old family called the Great Star by another name, theirs was 'Nyota-Kuu.' Which one's right?"

"Well," smiled Ushomi, "I don't think the Great One cares what you call Him. He cares for all meerkats, you know."

"But if that were true... why do we fight each other?"

"That's out of His hands. Families have to settle their differences on their own."

"But why can't we all get along?" asked the inquisitive youngster. "I mean, there's plenty of land here for all of us, isn't there?"

Ushomi leaned toward the pup, sensing that he was troubled. "Something's eating you, Masada. What is it?"

Masada bowed his head in sorrow. "My Family's still out there —not this family, the other one. I dunno if I'll ever see them again, but if I do... I don't wanna fight them." For once, Ushomi was at a loss for words.

Imbali, Tamu and Abeni came out from their hiding places to cuddle and console their new brother. "Don't worry Masada," cooed Tamu, "you still got us." "Besides," added Abeni, "if your family really did attack you, they'd be crazy!"

Masada sighed. Maybe they were right; maybe the Kivuli clan was a thousand miles away now. Maybe they had forgotten all about him. Maybe he would never see them again, and they would be nothing more than a happy memory.

If only he was right.

"Intruders!" cried out Zola. "We're under attack!"

Busara wasted no time in flushing out the Isibani clan with the help of her daughters Naima, Tani and Haraka. The ones they ran into were Gamba, Zarina and Zola, as they were foraging on open sand. The attack was swift. Busara, leading the charge, went straight into Zarina while Tani and Haraka ganged up on Gamba. That left Naima, who was barely a month old, facing off against Zola.

The older female sized up her rival and scoffed, "Huh! A bit short for a warrior, aren't you?"

"Go on, do your worst you great big bully!" shouted Naima.

"Don't tempt me," hissed Zola with bared teeth.

Naima was small, but she had a strategy. She let Zola chase her around so that they would collide with two others from another side of the battlefield. Sure enough, it worked; Naima nimbly dodged Gamba and sent Zola jumping right onto him. And just to add insult to injury, Naima snuck up behind the dazed Zola and bit her tail.

"Augh! That sneaky brat!" shouted Zola. Gamba forced himself up and recovered quickly. "Zola, help your sister!"

Zarina had her claws full with the team-up of Busara and Tani. She was getting scratched and bitten left and right, but they were only minor injuries. Gamba and Zola hurried to push off their leader's oppressors before they could do serious damage.

"Isibani... Retreat!" Zarina panted.

Zarina and her small gang had no choice but to run; they were terribly outnumbered. Even Zola could see that and wouldn't accuse anyone of cowardice this time. Zarina took them several feet out, then stopped to see if the enemy was following. She was amazed to see that they weren't.

Instead, Busara stood her ground, taller than her daughters, and shouted out loud and clear: "If you value your lives and your children, leave now and never come back!"

Getting the message, Zarina slowly led her gang away. But just as they found their stride, the Isibani queen grew fearful again. "They just threatened our little ones."

"Should we make it back home?" asked Zola.

"If they know where we live," gulped Zarina, "then we may already be too late."

The Isibani picked up the pace for home.

Busara would have been satisfied with her scare tactic, but not Shujaa. Shujaa wanted blood. He would only feel victory in his grasp if he were to kill at least one rival. Just one was all he needed. He would get his chance in Wetland.

While Ushomi and his little charges stared in awe at passing giraffes, Shujaa and his sons had spotted them from a far distance. Despite the gap between the two groups, the eyes of the Kivuli were as sharp as ever. "One adult... Four pups," observed Shujaa.

"Hardly good odds for them," grinned Kucha sinisterly.

"Hardly a fair fight, wouldn't you say?" protested Makali. "They're only children."

"Would you rather wait 'till they're all grown up?" replied Jino.

Shujaa then spoke up, "This is war, Makali; all are accountable, even the weak. Do you understand?"

"Yes, Father." Makali bowed his head, but remained reluctant.

"Jino, Kucha, follow them back to the burrow," commanded the patriarch. "Jasiri, Makali, we will search for any other stragglers. We will all meet up at the enemy's doorstep."

"Yes sir!" replied the group.

Just as Shujaa had planned, his sons quietly stalked Ushomi and the pups all the way to the edge of Fell Tree – a secondary home of the Isibani. It was named after the old shattered tree stump that at one point in history was a tower. All that remained of the once proud tree were scattered logs and a hollow husk that worked as a useful bolt hole.

Ushomi's ears picked up the sound of crackling grass from behind and immediately sensed danger, just as he and the pups neared the old stump. He stopped in his tracks.

"Ushomi?" peeped a concerned Masada. "What's wr--"

"Shh... We're being followed," whispered Ushomi. "Don't look back, just keep going forward. Pick up the pace, kids..."

The frightened pups did as they were told and began to trot.

"Faster," murmured Ushomi, sensing the approaching enemies. "Don't look kids, just head for home... Faster... Run! RUN!"

Jino and Kucha charged out of their hiding places and straight for the Isibani. There were only two of them, but they were twice as fast as the pups. Ushomi had only one option: to take Jino and Kucha head on. He skidded to a halt, turned around and tackled Kucha, who was completely taken by surprise.

"Ushomi!" gasped Masada, who stood at the foot of the getaway burrow they were headed for.

"Run, Masada! Hide! Go now!" screamed Ushomi, who was soon counter-attacked by Jino.

Masada had no choice but to obey and disappeared into the burrow along with his sisters.

Though Ushomi was outnumbered, he was a skillful fighter and proved it by holding Jino's ear with his teeth while at the same time scratching Kucha's face with his back paws. As soon as his attackers were stunned, he broke free of them and jumped into the burrow.

Jino and Kucha, their pride more sore than their wounds, paced around the burrow entrance intently. "Just wait, you trespassers!" called out Jino. "When our father gets here, you'll wish you never set foot in our land!"

"Hurry, kids! Go as far as you can," coaxed Ushomi, as he and the pups rushed down a dark and seemingly endless hole. "Don't stop until you reach a dead end."

While losing their breath, the pups treaded on. "Who are they, Ushomi?" panted Imbali. "Why are they after us?"

Don't worry kids," assured the elder. "We can wait down here until our family comes home. Then we'll be saved."

"Isn't Imbasa-Kulu gonna throw down his thunderbolt?" asked Abeni.

"Imbasa-Kulu doesn't play favorites," replied Masada.

"He's right," frowned Ushomi. "All we can do is go as far down as we can... and pray for a miracle."

Shujaa was not an evil meerkat. He wasn't heartless at all; he had a family, and loved them as dearly as any father should. But when on a warpath, he could prove to be quite vicious. He was horrified and furious to find his sworn enemies nesting in a burrow that once belonged to the Kivuli. In Shujaa's mind, it still belonged to them. "How dare they," he growled under his breath, as he and his sons followed Kucha and Jino's directions.

"They're less than a mile from our home," Jasiri observed fearfully.

Shujaa bared his teeth. "Come. We finish this once and for all. Whether they're small babes or full-grown warriors, we'll leave none alive. Attack!"

Three hot-blooded Kivuli males dove into the opening of the small burrow and quickly went to work on widening the entrance, so that the whole marauding party could enter at one time. The mission caused a puff of smoke to rise up from shoveled sand, but the Kivuli weren't concerned about drawing attention to themselves. Perhaps they should have been.

Heading home with a steady pace were the Isibani twins Anguka and Choma. They were excited to bring their family news about a burrow they had found some miles away from the Kivuli. Imagine their horror upon seeing smoke in the distance, in the direction where Fell Tree burrow was.

The twins charged toward home, but stopped short upon realizing what was causing the smoke. Clearly, their home was under siege, and because there were only two of them, their options were limited.

The boys needed only to glance at each other, and without saying a word, they agreed to go and fetch reinforcements. They sped off before any of the marauders noticed their presence. In only two minutes, the burrow's entrance opened up for Shujaa and Jasiri.

"This is it, son," said Shujaa. "You boys keep watch; Jasiri and I will finish this!" As the elder males climbed into the tunnel, Jino and the others began to assert themselves as the rightful owners of Fell Tree.

The pups, terrified as they were, followed their big brother Ushomi down dozens of corridors until at last they hit a dead end.

"We're trapped," panted Abeni.

"How far down are we?" wondered Tamu.

"Far enough to feel cold," shivered Imbali.

Ushomi gathered the little ones into a huddle, both to warm them and comfort them. While they savored a moment of peace, Ushomi prepared for the worst. "Listen to me, kids. This is where you have to stay until you're saved. You're not to move from this spot, or make any sound. Do you kids understand?"

"Uh-huh," they all murmured.

"I need you kids to really trust me now."

Masada turned around to look Ushomi in the eyes. "...
What's going on, Ushomi?"

"You kids have to be brave now..." With that, he finally
let go of the pups and began to back away.

"Ushomi!" gasped Masada. "Where are you going?"

"I'm going to stop them from finding you."

"...But--"

"Don't move. Don't make a sound."

"...Ushomi?"

"Trust me, kids..." Then he turned toward the long hall
back toward the surface, and left.

Of the bewildered pups, Masada was the most horrified.
Was Ushomi really going to take a whole gang of rivals by
himself!? Was he insane? ...Or could he really do it? The
little pup couldn't bear to stay hidden and wait for answers.
But he knew he had no choice; his little sisters were now
shivering with fear, more-so than cold. He decided to lean
on them in hopes to silence their soft moans.

The sad truth, Ushomi was at a complete disadvantage.
Not only were Shujaa and Jasiri bigger and stronger than he,
but they were now plowing deeper into the tunnels, knowing
it like the back of their paws. Still, Ushomi was ready. If this
were to be his last stand, he would die honorably. Jasiri was
all too ready to grant Ushomi such an honor.

As soon as the two young warriors faced each other,
Jasiri tore into the enemy as if he were prey. His teeth
clutched tightly onto Ushomi's face, but the brave Isibani
shook vigorously until he was left with bloody scratches on
his nose.

Ushomi gave as best as he had gotten by latching onto
Jasiri's left ear. It was now Jasiri's turn to shake like a rag

doll, but upon the final jolt, a piece of his ear ripped off. He didn't even have time to yelp in pain, because Ushomi was now pinning him down.

"Keep him busy, son!" barked Shujaa.

Finally, this was Shujaa's moment to conquer. He weaved right past the distracted Ushomi and proceeded to stalk toward the burrow's lowest level. There, he would be met with a most unexpected surprise.

The pups did their best to stay quiet and hidden, but soon they heard soft footsteps approaching.

"Someone's coming," whispered Abeni fearfully.

"Sh!" hushed Imbali. "Don't make a sound."

Quietly, Masada stuck his nose in the air. He could smell the oncoming stranger's scent, but something about this scent disturbed him... It was familiar! All at once, it hit him; this was the scent of the Kivuli clan, the family he once believed he'd never seen again. And no other Kivuli smelled as strongly as this one: "Dad..."

Masada's heart sank with immense sorrow; he no longer felt fear of any kind but a strong will to set things right. He tore himself away from his sisters and bravely headed for the hallway. None of their soft begs could bring him back to them. The young pup almost marched upward, toward his oncoming opponent. He was convinced that once his father heard his voice, the attack would cease.

But then, all too quickly, Masada found himself face to face with a Shujaa he had never seen before. His eyes glowed with intent to kill. His teeth were bared like those of an Anubis. Upon seeing the pup, Shujaa gave out a sound so eerie, so unlike a meerkat, that it was as though he borrowed the Wadjet's hiss.

Masada was now more terrified than ever, but he stood his ground. "Dad! Dad, stop! It's me! It's Masada!" he yelled.

Shujaa growled furiously.

"Daddy, it's me— Masada! I'm your son! Don't you recognize me!?"

Poor Masada. He was too naive to understand the situation. In complete darkness, a meerkat can and often does rely completely on his sense of smell. And as far as Shujaa's nose was concerned, this pup standing in front of him smelled like an Isibani.

"Do you think me a fool, little worm?" Shujaa growled.

"W-worm? ...D-dad, it's me!"

"You lie! Your feeble attempt to trick me is useless, puny scum!"

Masada was at a loss; petrified, he wasn't sure what to do next. He only had one plan, and that plan failed. Shujaa then threw his claws down on the helpless pup, readying his fangs to press down on him as he squirmed.

"What I do now, I do for the sake of my family."

"And what I do now," called out Ushomi's voice, "is for the sake of MINE!"

Ushomi came flying out of nowhere and tackled Shujaa, knocking him down.

"Run, Masada!" called out the pup's hero. "Run! Don't look back, just run!" Masada had no other choice but to do as he was told; he went running in the direction of his sisters while Ushomi did his best against the Kivuli clan's Champion.

After twenty-five minutes, the Kivuli boys continued to open up entrances to Fell Tree's underground lair. The day seemed to be theirs, until they heard an unpleasant war cry in the distance.

It was the Isibani, in full force, charging wildly toward the burrow. The young Kivuli males had very little time to counter the attack. Anguka and Choma matched strengths with Jino and Choma. Zarina and Zola tore into Makali. Gamba, king of the Isibani, flew into the burrow to secure whoever was still alive inside.

Inside the tunnels, a battle-scarred Jasiri could hear enemy footsteps approaching. Panic-stricken, he dashed down to where Shujaa was already tearing Ushomi apart.

"Father, Father! The enemy's back! We must retreat!"

Shujaa, already weakened from battle, decided to heed his son's advice. Together, they left the burrow in shambles.

Once daylight was in their faces again, Shujaa and Jasiri quickly regrouped the Kivuli clan.

"Onward home, my sons! Onward home!" exclaimed Shujaa.

With that, the Kivuli boys took off like a hurricane, leaving a trail of dust and destruction in their wake.

All was suddenly quiet in the bowels of Fell Tree burrow. In fact, it was too quiet. Masada nuzzled his terror-frozen sisters and murmured, "I think they're gone."

"How do you know?" whispered Tamu nervously.

"Because it's quiet."

"Did they see you?" asked Imbali softly.

Masada was hesitant to reply; instead, he opened his ears and listened for other voices.

Then at last, he heard something. "Listen... You hear that? ...It's Gamba! We're saved!"

Indeed, it was Gamba's voice calling to them. The pups rejoiced and hurried into the tunnel halls to find their father. All but one.

Masada slowly and cautiously followed the fresh smell of blood in the dirt and on the walls. He knew where and to whom the trail would lead.

"Ushomi? ...Ushomi, where are you?" he faintly called out.

There were no answers to his call, but that didn't stop his search or his hope. Soon enough, Masada did indeed find his older brother, but wasn't prepared to see Ushomi's horrible wounds. His neck was especially damaged, making blood spill out onto his fur to the point were he seemed unrecognizable. It was fortunate for the pup that his vision was blurred by the darkness; he couldn't see just how far gone Ushomi was.

"Ushomi?" Masada muttered as he moved closer.

Ushomi lay on his side, too weak to move except for his face. He could sense Masada's presence and forced a smile. "Hey..." he whispered. "You're safe..."

Masada tried to hold back tears as he begged, "Come on, get up Ushomi. We gotta get outta here."

"...I... I can't..." Ushomi's breath began to die down.

"Please, Ushomi. We need you... Please don't..."

"Be brave, little guy. Whatever happens, just be brave."

"Masada?" cried out Zarina's voice in the distance. "Ushomi! Masada!"

"Your mother's calling you," smiled Ushomi weakly. "Go to her."

"Ushomi..." Once again, Masada was being forced to leave his hero by rejoining the family. He gave Ushomi a soft and meaningful nuzzle before creeping out of the hole he was lying in.

Masada looked back on Ushomi one last time, showing his reluctance to leave. "Be brave," whispered Ushomi. Masada gave him a quiet nod, and walked away.

Upon seeing her surrogate son approaching, Zarina gasped with joy; "Masada! Oh, thank the stars you're alive."

While his daughter flung her arms around the shaken pup, Gamba ventured further down the tunnel in hopes his own son. When at last he did find Ushomi it was already too late.

Gamba fell back in horror at the sight of his torn and bloodied offspring. "My son! ...O, my poor son," he grieved. He took a moment to rest his head on Ushomi's body and let the tears fall.

The whole Isibani clan would have their time to grieve for heroic Ushomi, but first they had to move. When everyone felt strong enough, they picked up their feet and followed Anguka and Choma to a new burrow.

The journey toward Squirrel Patch took longer had there been no casualties that day. The Isibani kept a slow pace on account of their grief for Ushomi. Young Abeni struck up a song in hopes to revitalize everyone's spirits, and soon they all joined her:

> *"My heart is so heavy, each beat takes a day.*
> *My mind is so weary, all my thoughts drift away.*
> *I am beaten, I am broken, my strength is all but gone.*
> *Yet I move on, yet I move on.*
>
> *"My tears fall like torrents, I may drown in my steps.*
> *My feet feel like anvils, though I can't afford to rest.*

I am lost and I'm forsaken, my hopes have all been wronged
Still I move on, still I move on.

"There's hope there in the distance, though it may seem too
far. There's no path to be taken, so we follow all the stars.
We are helpless, we are homeless, but that can't last for too
long.
So I move on, so I move on."

Squirrel Patch was home to a large troop of ground squirrels, creatures unlike meerkats except for their equal affinity with burrows. These neighbors would prove to be far friendlier than the Kivuli. By the time the Isibani arrived there, it was dusk. The clan gathered together to comfort each other in light of their losses. For the most part, their voices were silent. But not for long.

Zola, the defiant littermate of Zarina, was so engulfed with fury that she could bottle it up no longer. "Cowards... That's what they are! Only a wretched coward would attack a burrow full of helpless pups! If it weren't for Ushomi, we would have lost Abeni. Or Imbali. Or Tamu. Or..." She then eyed Masada, and all at once she found a target for her vengeful anger. "You. You're not one of us. You never were!"

"Zola," hissed Zarina nearby.

"I told you, sister. I told you this one would bring a curse upon us. And now you see what happens?"

"Stop it, Zola! This was not Masada's fault!"

"That's enough, Zola!" barked Zarina.

But the damage had been done. Masada heard everything and was so heartbroken that he fled the scene. Zarina saw this and growled at her sister Zola. "Now see what you've done? Shame on you!" She then took off after her distraught pup.

"Masada... Masada, wait!" Zarina panted as she blocked his way. "Don't listen to Zola, she's wrong about you."

"No," he sniffed in despair. "She's right. I am a curse. I killed Ushomi just like I killed my brother."

"What do you mean?"

"Before I met you," he explained tearfully, "I had a brother named Kivuli... I went chasing after the Great Star and then there was a big- ...He-he followed me."

"Hush, dear. Take your time."

"...Kivuli followed me. We ran into an Anubis. I jumped into a hole, and then... then... it got 'im."

"Oh sweetheart," cooed Zarina as she hugged him; "That wasn't your fault. None of this is your fault."

"Then why do I feel so guilty?" sniffed Masada.

"Do you remember what I told you the day we met?" asked Zarina gently. "Life gives us many tests, and we can only pass them by being strong and by staying as a family."

"But Zola--"

"Zola will understand someday. She may even accept you someday. But no matter what anybody says, you are one of us, Masada. And you are special." While snuggling up to her under her arm, Masada began to feel at peace, just as he did when they first met. Zarina seemed to know exactly what to say. She was proving to be an excellent mother.

But after seeing his biological father, Masada began to see things differently. Rivals were no longer evil in his eyes. There was only one true evil in the world: indifference. He vowed to himself that he would somehow end this war, even if it were to cost him his own life.

It would be two more years before he could put himself to the test.

9

Green grass was turning to brown almost too quickly for the Isibani. They had settled into a quiet patch and had gone undetected by their rivals, the Kivuli, for some time. But now that the seasons were changing, a new threat was looming. The gang kept vigilance against tall amber grass in hopes to find soft soil or spot danger.

Standing almost as tall as the rest of them was Masada. He was now two years old; mature enough to perhaps father his own pups, but still young at heart to accept his subordinate role. And by now, just as he hoped, even strong-willed Zola had accepted him as part of the family.

"The wind's picking up," observed Gamba. "We can't find anything in this, kids. Let's head back."

The clan struggled as the wind blew dust and debris in their faces, while the grass whipped back and forth like waves on a restless sea. Going home on empty bellies and lashed faces was not an ideal scenario for the group, but what awaited them at home would surely lift their spirits.

Zarina was not fortunate enough to have a mate that would settle down with her, but in time she was at least blessed with four pups of her own. They were three boys; Isibandi ("Courage"), Umoya ("Wind"), Ubani ("Lightning"), and a girl, Tundi ("Hope"). At four weeks old, they were nearly ready to leave the safety of their burrow, but as long as the grassland hid countless dangers, it was best for them to wait for their dinner.

Imbali, now a mature adult, was their baby-sitter for the day. All was peaceful at the burrow, until Imbali heard the sound of paw prints of a meerkat approaching. At first she assumed her family was returning from the foraging, but soon she would find out that someone actually beat them to the punch.

It's perfectly normal for a male meerkat who has come of age to leave his immediate family in hopes to start one of his own. Imbali was soon in the presence of one such amorous bachelor. The young lady-kat wasn't taking chances and hurried her toddler charges into the burrow. Even a lone stranger could be dangerous.

But not this one. He stood tall on his hind legs as if trying to look impressive. "Good afternoon!" He smiled. "Are you the lady of the household?"

Nervous, Imbali checked to see if the stranger was addressing her. She looked left and right, but there was only she and the bachelor. "Me? Oh, no! I'm not the head of the family. I'm just babys-" She clasped tightly onto her mouth, realizing she may have just endangered the pups.

"Don't worry," chuckled the stranger. "It's not pups I'm looking for. You tell whoever your queen is that I'm in the neighborhood, won't you? The name's Makuu."

"What do you want with our queen?" asked Imbali suspiciously.

"Oh," stretched the youthful male, "you're too young to understand. Just drop my name to her, won't you? There's a good girl... Makuu!"

"Right. Got it: Makuu."

"Okay! Take care!" cheered the young bachelor, and scampered off after hearing paw steps approaching.

As if on cue, the family returned just as the bold young male took off in the opposite direction.

Imbali's fur stood on end and she shook her head in disgust. "Brr! The nerve of some guys."

"What guys?" asked Masada as he skid up to her.

"This guy named Makuu just came around asking for Zarina. He was really smug about it too, strutting around like he owned the place."

The twins Anguka and Choma stood up in response, "You tell us when he comes back, sis, and we'll come runnin'!"

"Yeah! He'll strut on over, but he'll go limpin' back."

Zola couldn't help but enter the conversation, "Isn't it Zarina's decision to let rovers near? She is, after all, a queen without a king."

"Who needs a new king when we've got dad?" One of the twins responded defiantly.

Zola rolled her eyes. "Do we have to explain the whole procreation deal again?"

The boys replied with gross-out faces.

"I hoped not," sighed Zola.

"Zola has a point though," said Masada nearby. "Maybe we should give Makuu a chance. I mean, what's the harm in it?"

"Bro," said one of the twins harshly, "You want dad to leave!?"

"You realize that if Zarina picks a bachelor and he stays, that means dad has to leave us for good?" asked the other twin.

"Whatcha got against dad anyway?"

"Yeah! What's with you all of a sudden?"

"Guys! Guys!" shouted Masada. "I've got nothing against Gamba! He's a great leader."

"He's the best!"

"I know he's the best, Choma... Anguka?"

The twins giggled in satisfaction; they'd rather not let anyone guess which twin was which; and left Masada anguish in embarrassment. "Alright, seriously now!" huffed the young male. "Which one of you is which? No games this time, just the flat out truth."

At first, the feisty twins agreed to cooperate:

"I'm Anguka."

"I'm Choma."

"Thank you," nodded the relieved Masada.

Then the look-alikes ran circles around each other, which caught Masada completely off guard. Finally, they stopped in the same place, only now there was no way of telling whether they had switched places or not.

"Now which are we?" they laughed in unison.

Masada made a face at them; he gave up.

"Hey! Red alert!" barked Zola nearby. "Someone's in the brush."

While the gang prepared for a showdown, they would soon realize that just like Makuu this stranger was no immediate threat. Instead, he had interests only in an available female. This time, the bachelor looking for love was none other than Masada's biological brother, Makali! It had been a fairly long while since the two blood relatives had seen each other, and so the sad fact was that Masada could see this new arrival as only a stranger.

Unlike his rival, the wily Makuu, Makali thought it best to keep a low profile and hide behind a wall of grass. His cover was already blown thanks to Zola, but by lying flat on his back, he was proving to be harmless. But Gamba, who had been the head of the family for so long, found it hard to pass down his leadership. Harmless or not, Makali had to go.

The shy male stayed hidden in the grass, focusing intently on Zarina as she stood atop a tall mound of soil. The young queen eyed him curiously. She had been romanced once before, but this bachelor was different. The suave gleam in his eye told her that he meant to stay. This made her smile; at last, she thought, a father for her children. She descended from her throne for a closer look.

Seeing her move made Makali excited. He paused to quickly groom himself to look more presentable. But just as he leaned forward, he was welcomed by a very different meerkat: Gamba!

"Yaiyee!!"

Makali jumped out of the grass like a bat out of hell and made chase, with the overprotective Gamba close behind. His sons cheered wildly as Gamba forced his rival to make circles around the den. Then finally, the scared-witless Makali took off toward the high dunes in the distance, indicating his complete departure from their territory.

Gamba let his rival escape, satisfied that his kingship was secure. He was then surrounded by his admiring children — all but one. Zarina reclaimed her place on the mound, looking down on her father with a look of deep disappointment. Gamba noticed her sad frown, and suddenly felt guilty about his actions.

"Over there!" barked Imbali, seeing a distant stranger standing tall near the dunes. "Another intruder!"

"I'll get him!" announced Masada, and the young male charged ahead of Gamba. Masada, inspired by his foster father's fearlessness, felt the need to take action against all rovers who would dare to sever the family's bonds.

The distant meerkat took off for the dunes, just as Makali did earlier. What lie beyond those great sand hills was a mystery to the Isibani clan. Yet Masada pressed on with increased determination. When he reached the top of the orange dune, he paused to observe the vast green pasture that lay beyond it. In Masada's eyes, he seemed to have stumbled upon a gold mine. And it was right in his own backyard!

He then spotted the retreating stranger, who lost a lot of ground to cover after sliding down the dune. Masada would have this intruder in his grasp; all he had to do was slide down as skillfully as possible. By taking a flying leap, he belly-flopped halfway down and gravity pulled him straight to the ground.

The stranger darted into a tree log in desperation; there were no bolt holes in sight. But now she was cornered, with no way out. She curled into a ball and silently prayed for a miracle.

Masada quickly approached the log, seeing that he had the upper hand. "You there!" he called. "There's nowhere left to run, so you might as well surrender."

"Surrender means death," responded the female.

Masada gasped in surprise; up until now, he thought he was chasing an amorous rover. "Who are you?" he asked calmly.

He was stunned by her reply: I am Naima of the Kivuli clan. I meant no harm in coming here."

"... Naima?" echoed the young male.

"Yes."

"... Let me look at you. Come on out."

"Oh, no! I'm not falling for that!"

"Naima, it's me! Masada!"

The young female, the same age as her pursuer, turned her head around to see this stranger's face. "I... I had a brother with that name."

"I'm him. He's me. Don't you see? I am your brother."

"No! You lie!" she backed away from him fearfully.

"Please," begged the young male. "Please hear me out. Our parents are Shujaa and Busara. You and I had a littermate named Kivuli. We worshipped Nyota-Kuu. We were separated when we were pups... What more proof do you need?"

Stunned and shaken, Naima slowly crept out of her hiding place, her eyes focused heavily on the stranger's face.

He did indeed look familiar – like family. "...Bless my eyes, lest they deceive me... Masada?" The young male nodded happily. Before he knew it, he and his twin sister were embracing and nuzzling.

Tender as this moment was, it did not last long. Someone else was in the area, and he was horrified to see his little sister being held in the arms of a total stranger. Jasiri's eyes beamed with growing rage.

Naima paused to clear her thoughts and senses. "... What happened to you, Masada? Where have you been all this time?"

Said the equally emotional Masada, "I've been adopted by the Isibani. They're really good people, they've treated me like one of their own."

"But... Masada, we're your family. You should have come back." Masada's littermate rubbed her nose. "... Gosh, look at you. You're so big and...handsome." Masada couldn't help but blush.

"Mom and Dad would be so proud," added Naima, "if only they-"

"Hey! You!!" barked a tall, menacing-looking male nearby. "Get your filthy paws off my little sister!"

Masada was completely awestruck by this character; part of his left ear was chewed off, a reminder of his fight against an enemy during a burrow raid two years earlier.

"Jasiri!" gasped Naima. She jumped in between the two males defensively; "It's okay, Jasiri, he's one of us!"

"Get out of here, Naima. Let me handle this."

"But you don't understand! He's-"

"**Rawr!**" Jasiri lunged.

77

Masada had no choice but to push Naima out of the way and let Jasiri tackle him. They tussled, growled, spat and clawed, but Masada was too swift and agile for his older brother. He managed to squirm out of Jasiri's grip, and tried to make a run for the sand dunes.

"Jasiri, no! Stop!" cried out Naima, but her pleas would fall on deaf ears. Jasiri tore across the plain and caught up with Masada within moments. This time, Jasiri pinned down his enemy with his sharp fangs. Masada never felt such sudden pain; it was as if Jasiri was really an Anubis in disguise. The older meerkat clenched onto his neck, nearly strangling him. The more he struggled, the harder Masada found it to breathe. In one brief act of desperation, he lifted his right paw, claws ready, and dug them into Jasiri's face.

Masada had proven to be much stronger than he seemed; Jasiri roared in pain and lifted himself over his foe. The younger meerkat backed away quickly, and saw that Jasiri's face was now bleeding. Shock overtook him for a moment, but soon he heard his sister cry out: "Masada! Run!"

Masada took a deep breath and flew like the wind toward the great sand dunes, leaving his brother and sister behind.

Naima watched as Jasiri hunched over in agony. She gulped worriedly, as Makali and Tani came running.

"We heard screams," panted Tani.

"What happened?"

"Tani. Makali..." Naima sputtered. "It's Masada."

"Huh?" blinked Makali.

"Masada's alive. I just saw him."

Then a bitter Jasiri came forward and growled, "He was not our brother, Naima. He tried to take advantage of you."

"No Jasiri. It is him! I know it."

"Naima, look at me!" hissed Jasiri, forcing her to gaze at his scratched and bloodied cheek. "No brother of ours would do this."

Naima's heart sank; she could no longer defend Masada.

"Come," murmured the injured one, "we've got to warn the others. This place is no longer safe."

Tani, Makali, and even Naima followed Jasiri's lead. But Naima had to take one last look at the dunes before leaving them behind. In her heart, she prayed that this wouldn't be her last meeting with her long-lost brother Masada.

Masada, likewise, had to return to the Isibani burrow and warn about the Kivuli's claim of Dune Valley. He felt guilty about wounding his brother, but he knew he had no other choice. He could only hope that his actions would not shatter his chances of making peace with the Kivuli.

10

A storm was brewing on the horizon, but it promised no rain; only cold air, dry sand, and starving meerkats. A very different kind of storm was brewing at the Kivuli burrow, for Naima was about to face the wrath of her parents. She sat up before them, while her siblings – now eleven in total – kept a safe distance from her.

Busara and Shujaa stood up on their hind paws atop a small dune, making them look even more formidable than they already were.

"Naima," said Busara sternly; "is it true that you were found with a male stranger yesterday?"

Naima, frightened as she was at seeing how angry her parents were, kept surprisingly calm. "He's not a stranger, Mother. He's my brother Masada – the one taken from us during the Dark Day."

"Impossible," growled Shujaa. "Masada was killed that day, and will never return."

"But Father," argued Naima, "I saw him with my own eyes. I would know if it were him or not."

"Naima, you were only a pup when Masada was killed."

"Even so, Father..."

"Then," Busara asked firmly, "why is it that this 'Masada,' the one you saw yesterday, attacked your brother Jasiri?" Naima couldn't help but glance at where Jasiri sat. His face, battle worn and scarred, turned away in shame. Naima faced her parents once again. "Jasiri was the one who started the fight. He didn't give Masada a chance to explain himself."

Shujaa then replied, "Jasiri saw you and that stranger snuggling. That was his statement."

"It was only-"

"Were you or were you not cuddling up to a roving male yesterday, Naima?"

"No!"

"Don't lie to me!"

"Shujaa, enough!" barked queen Busara. She then descended from the slope and looked Naima deeply in the eyes. Her voice was gentle, albeit threatening: "Naima, child, I can forgive you for being young and naive. But to go behind my back and choose your own mate, while you're still under my rule, is a personal offense-"

"Mother-"

"Let me finish, child... A crime like that would lead you to exile and banishment from this family. Now, look into my eyes and tell me truthfully. Were your intentions with this stranger innocent or not?"

Naima's eyes glazed with pity. "Mother... It was my brother. It really, truly was."

Busara saw what she needed to see in her daughter's honest eyes.

"Treachery!" cried out Shujaa from his throne of sand. "She speaks madness! Busara, send her away!"

"No!" cried out Naima fearfully.

"I will deal with her alone, Shujaa," said Busara as she nudged Naima. "The rest of you go your own way. This case is closed." With that, Shujaa and his subordinates left the area in one direction, while Busara led Naima in the opposite direction. They were all certain what her verdict was.

When they were at last alone, Busara heard her young daughter's faint whimpers. She sighed deeply. "Mother, please," begged Naima softly, "please don't send me away. I meant what I said."

Busara then looked her in the eyes again; this time, there wasn't a smidge of aggression in her. "I believe you, Naima... I know you would never betray me."

Naima was stunned. "... You. You b-believe me?"

"Listen, Naima," said her mother softly, as if secretly. "I never said this to anyone, but when your Father came home from a burrow raid long ago, he told me something that I'll never forget."

"What did he say?"

"He said that one of the enemy pups he ran into called him 'Daddy.' He said... that pup called himself Masada."

Naima gasped with both shock and awe.

"I didn't want to discuss it with him further; I was still very upset about losing two of my pups."

"I understand."

"But when you said you've met Masada, all of a sudden I remembered it... I'm beginning to see the truth now. Masada... is alive."

"Oh, Mom!" chirped Naima, as she embraced Busara joyfully. "We've got to tell the others," cheered Naima. "They have to know!"

"No, child," replied Busara solemnly. "It won't change anything."

"What? But Mom..."

"Even if he is our Masada," explained Busara with a frown, "we cannot undo what's happened. He belongs to the others now."

"He belongs with us," Naima argued.

"It is not up to us, dear. Only Masada can choose where he belongs."

Naima needed to take a moment to let her mother's wise words sink in. As badly as she wanted Masada back, her mother knew better. It just wasn't that simple.

"Come now, Naima, don't be upset." Busara cooed. "Knowing our boy is alive and grown is enough cause for celebration. And as for the others..."

"Like Father?"

"Yes...Shujaa will only believe what his heart tells him, and I know that in his heart, Masada is dead. He and the others will just have to see the truth for themselves."

"Oh, if you could see him, Mother..." smiled Naima. The queen returned the smile. "The day I see my Masada again will be the brightest day of my life." They embraced lovingly again, letting the embrace be the final say in their discussion.

Busara gave herself a moment to absorb all of her emotions – shock, joy, pain, and most of all, relief. But most importantly, she gave herself a moment to look straight up into the sky, at the sun for which she had harbored so much anger, so much blame. She would never forget that it was the sun's total eclipse that doomed her sons Masada and Kivuli that heartbreaking day. Not since then had she eyed the sun again, until now. In that small, fleeting moment between her and her god, all was forgiven.

11

Sandstorms became more frequent within the following week. Insects and arachnids alike burrowed deep enough into the earth so that they were no longer on the meerkat menu. The time of the dry season had begun. Already the Kivuli clan was preparing to move to more fruitful lands, even if it meant abandoning their turfs entirely. The Isibani, on the other hand, were concerned with the issue of departure. As the newcomers on the land, they would have no idea which direction to go in for greener pastures.

One afternoon, both Zarina and Zola sat atop the burrow while the others lay down on softer sand. The two eldest of females went back and forth on what the best measure of action was to go with. They went at it for hours, until at last Zarina addressed the group:

"My children, Father, brothers and sisters. The Great One had blessed me with a vision this morning. He has shown me exactly where we should go from here. I remember every tree, every dune and every obstacle we must cross. But hear me out, everyone! We will see a new green land at the end of this journey – a land where the rains will flood the earth and give us food that can last a whole year!"

Zola had always doubted her sister's leadership, but this "dream" turned out to be the last straw. Boldly she asked, "And, just how far is this flooding land, Zarina?"

"It's far," admitted the leader, "but we can make it."

"And since when did Imbasa-Kulu plant dreams in our minds? Mother had no such visions."

"Look Zola, I can't explain it myself. But I know what I saw in my dream, and I know it's all real."

"And what obstacles did you envision, Zarina?" asked Gamba patiently.

"A dried river, full of deep, sticky mud. And a group of large hunters that I've never seen before. And a great field where a wall of meerkats stand before us."

Zola paused to think things over. "Hmm... River gorges and a clan stand-off I can believe, but what of these new hunters? What do they look like?"

Zarina gulped at the thought of the nightmarish creatures again. "They're big...Bigger than the Anubis. They have talons like a Horus, and fangs far greater than a Wadjet's. And there's more, the biggest one of them all... His head shone like the Great Star Himself."

The others mused over the thought of such a creature, but Zola took offense, as her views of Imbasa-Kulu were arguably stronger than most meerkats. "Zarina," she growled, "you speak blasphemy. Any creature of the earth or sky that poses as the Great One is either a demon or a false trickster!"

The young queen shook her head, "You don't understand, Zola; this creature wasn't really glowing... He... His fur sprouted from his head like star rays. But it wasn't quite the same."

"It sounds like a trap," frowned Zola. "We'd be wise to take a different route than the one you've foreseen."

"There is no other path to take!" Zarina growled, asserting her dominance. The two girls faced off for a moment, but then Gamba stepped in:

"We'll worry about the dream and its meanings another day. We have at least one day's worth of foraging out here; I suggest we make the most of it."

"Here, here!" called out a few of the boys.

Although the girls silently agreed on this, Zarina and Zola couldn't take their eyes off each other. It would seem their patience with one another was quickly running out.

That late afternoon, Masada was in charge of babysitting Zarina's pups. Like Ushomi before him, the young adult male was a favorite guardian to the four rambunctious youngsters. But keeping up with four when there's only one of you could prove difficult:

"Now Tundi, don't eat that flower. Umoya, Ubani, don't wander off. Isibandi! Let go of your sister's tail! Ub-Umoya! Don't bite! That's it, get over here. Here! Stop that! Tundi, I told you to... STOP!!"

Four adventurous pups paused to gaze up at an already worn out babysitter. They've run circles around him long enough. Now was the time for a break. "Okay," panted Masada, "There we go... Now, you kids up for a story?"

"Oo! Oo! Tell us a good one, Masada!" cheered the young rascals. "Tell the one about lightning again. Or the Great One's breath in the wind! Or the tree-eaters!"

"I'll tell you one you haven't heard before," smiled Masada, which seemed to put the wild pups at ease.

> *"There is an old tale that tells why we meerkat families are at war. It all started with two particular clans: The Stripes, and the Spots.*
> *"'See here neighbor,' said the Striped one said one day. 'The Great Star shines brightest on my side of the desert; therefore, He favors me most of all.'*
> *"'Now see here neighbor,' replied the Spotted, 'The Great Star brings more rain to my side of the desert, which gives us more food. He clearly favors me over you.'*

"Now children, which clan leader do you think was right?"

The pups smiled wisely, "Neither."

"That's right," nodded Masada.

"But the Great Star could not intervene in their argument; instead, He sent a messenger to settle the matter.

"'Dear friend,' said the Spotted to the messenger, 'Come over to my burrow and see that it's better than my neighbor's.'

"'No, no!' called out Striped. 'Come over to my burrow instead.'

Torn between the two, the messenger stood his ground in between the two clans' territories.

"Now, the messenger was a meerkat himself, and a forgetful one at that. As time went on, he had forgotten his promise to the Great Star, and instead of settling the quarrel, he added his own statement: 'Brothers, surely the Great Star favors me most of all, because He has spoken directly to me!' And so the arguments continued.

"The Great Star sent other meerkats to settle the argument, but they too felt they were more superior to the others after having spoken to the Great One Himself. What started out as a quarrel between two had soon swelled into a war of many. Finally, the Great One addressed them all with a great, booming voice:

"'See here, you fools! If you can't settle things with each other, then perhaps it's best you all go as far from each other as you can!'

"And so, it was decided. The Stripes moved his clan to where the Great Star shone brightest; The Spots moved to where the rains fell most; and the others moved even farther to where they could always be near the Great Star. And until the argument is at last settled, all meerkats have been born with both stripes and spots as a reminder of their ancestors' foolish arrogance."

"But Masada," said Tundi, "that didn't really settle anything!"

"That's the whole point to the story," replied her big brother. "Even now, meerkat clans from all over can't agree on which of them is more favored by the Great One. And so, until someone can come up with a better solution, we will always have to keep a safe distance from our neighbors."

Umoya was the first to pick up on a strange scent. He wheeled himself around to follow his nose, and came to a stop upon seeing a meerkat in the distance. "Hey!" he barked. "Someone's coming!"

Alarmed, Masada gasped, "Quick! Hide in the burrow in case it's an intruder!"

Just as Masada had feared, it was indeed an unrelated meerkat coming their way. Masada stood his ground bravely while his tiny charges bolted to the burrow. "Who goes there?" he growled.

Then he heard a strangely familiar voice: "Masada? Is that you?"

He was quick to reply, "Naima!"

He allowed his littermate to scamper right up to the burrow, though his concerns grew. "What are you doing here?" he asked worriedly. "The others may be back soon."

"I had to see you again," insisted the young female. "Are you here all alone?"

"Well, not exactly..." Masada instinctively glanced back at the burrow entrance, from which one of the pups' heads peeked out in curiosity.

"Oh," blinked Naima, "I see... Uh, well... I'll make this quick then. Come back with me to the Kivuli land. We all miss you."

"Really?" asked a doubtful Masada. "Does Jasiri miss me too?"

"... Well, he would if he knew who you were. But Mother knows, and I know. That should be reason enough to come home, isn't it?"

Masada hesitated for an answer. "Naima... Two years ago, I would have gone back with you in an instant. But now? ..."

Naima was dumbfounded. "... You're... you won't come back?"

"I can't," he frowned. "I just can't leave these pups all alone."

"Are they yours?" she quickly asked.

"No."

"Then why do you care?"

"Because they see me as their brother."

"You're my brother!" she cried out. The only thing that could stop her from going on was the sound of whimpering pups. Naima gulped, then sighed shamefully.

"Sister," smiled Masada reassuringly, "everything's going to work out. I just know it. Now, we're planning to move soon, but there's no way we can without crossing into Kivuli land. I'll have to face Mom and Dad sooner or later and when I do..."

"You wouldn't fight them, would you?"

"Of course not, fighting is what started all our troubles." Then Masada gave his sister a gentle nuzzle on the cheek. "No matter what happens, I'll make things right. You'll see."

With hardly any more words between them, Naima and Masada said their goodbyes, assuring themselves it wouldn't be for the last time.

As the pups slowly crept out of their hiding place, Tundi looked up to her guardian and asked, "Who was that lady, Masada?"

As he watched his littermate run off into the distance, Masada solemnly replied, "Don't worry, kids... She's a good neighbor."

An entirely different family drama was unfolding in the Isibani foraging patch. Against her sister's rules, Zola led a small group into Kivuli territory. They could smell fresh grubs in that forbidden area, and it proved to be irresistible. It was Imbali, Abeni and the identical twins Anguka and Choma who all reaped the rewards of following their stubborn sister. Scorpions and millipedes were torn from the earth with enthusiasm. But this lunch would be cut short.

Gamba, the eldest, appeared in the distance. He stood tall on his hind legs, looking straight ahead for danger. "Keep on your guard!" he cried out. "I spot a Horus on the move!" But his children didn't hear him.

Meanwhile, Zola was nibbling down on a millipede when Zarina approached her with a look of discontent. "What do you think you're doing?" growled Zarina.

With her mouth full, Zola mumbled, "Wassif wook wike M'm booing?"

Zarina stepped forward with a glare of warning. "This is enemy territory."

"Well," swallowed Zola, "they're not here. So that makes this spot fair game."

"We've already lost Ushomi because we came too close to the Kivuli. Are you really willing to risk that again?"

Zola stood up on all fours in defiance, "That was a completely different matter. They attacked our home."

"So now we attack them. Is that your plan, Zola?"

The younger of the sisters gave a grin. "Well now that you've said it, maybe we should take this land! It's only right, isn't it? I mean, since they've so carelessly left it alone..."

Zarina saw a glint in Zola's eyes that she had seen before, the look of mutiny. She growled, "I won't start another war, sister."

The glint shone brighter as Zola stared Zarina down. "Then maybe it's time for a new leader."

Everyone stopped what they were doing, already alarmed by the sudden fit of loud snaps and growls. Within moments, Zola and Zarina had an audience. The sparring sisters locked hips, keeping one from scent-marking the other, and pushed each other around to see who could out-wrestle the other.

In the heat of the fight, Zola let loose an old grudge she had on her sister: "I was appalled when Mother chose you!"

Zarina responded by shoving Zola into a dried brush. Outraged, Zola dared to take a bite out of her sister's ear, but Zarina countered quickly with a snap at Zola's nose.

As the girls sparred, their younger siblings cheered for their favorite contender, whoever that may have been. Only wise old Gamba kept his vigilance, and within minutes he spotted a real terror in the sky. "Horus! Horus!!" he barked loudly. "Raise yourselves, children! A sky hunter's upon us!"

Alarmed, Anguka and Choma were next to look upward. Sure enough, a great big eagle was circling above them. They could see its talons itching for a meal. "Horus! Horus! Run!" screamed the boys, and took off in mad panic.

Seeing their brothers run off, Abeni and Imbali followed. Only Zola and Zarina were left in the open.

By the time they heard the alarm, it was too late; Zola and Zarina were in striking range of the eagle. When they looked upward, all they could see was a winged shadow and talons reaching out to them. Zarina took flight first, with Zola close behind her, but only one of them would reach safety.

Minutes felt like hours as Gamba and his children sat quietly in a bolt hole, waiting for the coast to be clear. It was Abeni who popped her head out of the hole first, and slowly scanned the skies. "... All clear!" she chirped.

The group found their courage and crawled into the light again. While the others breathed sighs of relief, Gamba looked around for his two oldest daughters, Zola and Zarina. He boldly trotted back to the spot where the girls sparred, and saw that no one was there. "Zola! Zarina! Where are you!?" He called out. "Zola! Zarina!?"

"... Father..."

Gamba heard a whisper nearby. He followed it to a small ditch where he found Zola curled up and shaking. He jumped into the ditch and nuzzled her gently; "Zola dear. ...Where is your sister?"

Zola's eyes were no longer glimmering with pride. They were now glazed and teary, a manner of which Gamba had never seen in them before. With trembling paws, she replied.

"The... The Horus. He came after me. He was right on top of me; I swear I could feel his claws... Then I felt a great shove, and I rolled down here."

"Zarina. Where is Zarina?"

"... He... He wanted me, Father... But Z-Zarina... she pushed me out of the way..."

"No," trembled Gamba's voice. Overtaken by shock, he ran in circles, scanning the sky, and cried out for the one daughter he would never see again.

A special ceremony was held at the Isibani burrow that evening. The group gathered together to mourn their second leader – their third loss altogether. The younger ones cuddled each other as the elder ones gave them gentle grooming treatments.

Gamba stood before the whole clan like a priest at a funeral, and began to preach with a heavy heart. "As we say goodbye to our leader and dear sister Zarina, let us remember her as she was – patient, strong, and kind. And let us not hold a grudge against the Horus that took her; for as we must harvest the underground-dwellers, so must our hunters harvest us for their own sakes. We must remind ourselves that the Great One has a plan for all creatures, whether we understand it or not."

As Gamba continued his sermon, Masada kept to himself, away from the others. He had his own reasons to feel so heartbroken: it was Zarina who took him into this family. She was more than just his leader; she was his hero - his surrogate mother. He bowed his head, feeling alone in his grief.

But soon, he would lift his head again, seeing Zola pull herself away from the crowd and the burrow itself. Unsure of her actions, he followed her until she stopped at the edge of the home field. Thinking she was alone at last, Zola dipped her head toward the ground, and began to cry her eyes out.

Masada was surprised; never before had he seen such vulnerability in this, Zarina's one and only rival. It made him realize that Zola was not the cold-hearted brute she made herself out to be. She had gentleness after all. As special as this moment was for him, Masada was compelled to break the silence: "Ahem."

Zola let out a gasp and whipped herself around. Seeing that it was only Masada there with her, she narrowed her eyes. "What do you want?"

Masada replied softly, "It's okay. You don't have to act tough around me."

"Who says I'm acting?" lied Zola as she straightened up.

"It must have been awful... Seeing that Horus take her away like that. I could never imagine-"

"Don't you dare pretend like you're my friend!" she snapped defensively. "You don't know me at all, you... you no-account outsider!"

Masada couldn't help but smile. "Hm... Still trying to be strong for the rest of us, aren't you? Well you don't have to, Zola. We all miss Zarina."

"She was my sister, Masada, not yours!"

"Yes, she was. She was your sister."

"...And I... "

"Fought for her crown, I know."

" ...I... I never wanted... "

"Zola," murmured Masada as he inched closer. "It wasn't your fault."

Masada's warm words went straight from her ears into Zola's heart; so much emotion filled up inside her that she couldn't contain it any longer. Her eyes welled up again, and she let out a big sob. As she cried, Masada opened his arms to her; Zola fell into them in her grief. There they stood, two former enemies, holding each other in comfort. Such a sight to be seen brought new light to the evening stars. Meerkats everywhere would tell of the night that outshone all others.

12.

A new day, and a new world dawned on the Isibani. With Zarina gone, the heavy crown of leadership was passed down to Zola, and although she vied for it before, she was now feeling reluctant about it. She had always thought she would earn the title, but never like this. Her first order of business was to seek out the Kivuli, not to start a fight, but rather hope to claim what lands they had left unguarded. After hours of fruitless searching, the Isibani had reason to believe that their enemies had moved on... possibly for good.

Zola, Gamba, Masada and the twins found the old burrow in which the Kivuli once nested; now, it was completely deserted. "They must have anticipated the drought," Gamba guessed.

"Then perhaps it's time we moved on too," suggested Zola.

"Well said," agreed Father. "The winds are pushing southward; that's where we should go."

Then one of the twin boys spoke up. "Are we going to the place Zarina dreamed about?"

"Huh? What place?" blinked Gamba forgetfully.

"You know," explained Choma (or Anguka), "The one she saw in a vision. Giant hunters, a wall of meerkats."

"Oh," remembered Zola. "I know what you're talking about. But we don't know how to get there, or if it exists."

"Of course it does!" replied the other twin. "The Great Star Himself gave her the vision!"

"Guys," sighed Zola, "dreams are illusions; Zarina was probably confused."

The young boys both gave her a glare. "Oh sure," said one of them, "that's easy for you to say. You never agreed with her."

Zola's fur stood on end as she replied, "Well then why don't you lead us to the dream place, Choma? ...or Anguka?"

"Children, please." Gamba shuffled himself between the group in hopes to make peace. "Dream place or no, we are leaving before the drought gets worse. We head south tomorrow, so eat up while you can." Such was his final word on the matter, and the rest of the day was spent on hectic foraging.

The night would prove restless for Zola. For one thing, the sky was filled with the echoes of thunder from a storm half a mile away. For another thing, Zola's sleep was invaded by a terrible dream.

Perhaps it was the argument she had with her brothers earlier that sparked it, or maybe it was an intervention of fate. For whatever reason, Zola saw in her dream The Great Star Himself... and He had a face.

It wasn't the kind of face a meerkat would expect of their sun god, if they expected one at all. His eyes were dark as coal, and slanted as if half closed. His snout was short and his nose triangular with its tip facing downward. His lips curled around his nose with a crease in the center, not unlike a predator's. But what was most astounding were the beams of light glowing around Him; they seemed to be made of hair or fur, and flowed as if blown by a wind. He seemed to be looking straight at her, and slowly gaped open his mouth, ready to roar.

Zola quickly snapped out of her dream, panting and shaking. More thunder bellowed in the distance, but could still be heard even under the burrow. The new queen paused to shake off her fear until she was once again calm enough to fall back to sleep. She would never utter a word about this dream to her family.

The journey began early the next day, as soon as everyone warmed themselves in the sun. While the adults began to walk without protest, the young pups kept looking back at the burrow they were leaving behind.

"Where are we going?" Tundi asked Masada as she trotted beside him. "Someplace where there's plenty of food," he replied.

"Will we ever see this place again?" asked Isibandi nearby.

"Yes," nodded Masada, "Someday I'm sure we will."

"I hope so," frowned young Umoya. "I really liked it here."

By late afternoon, after aimless wandering had already began to take its toll on the families, the Isibani found themselves in front of a muddy stream. This was the remaining remnant of last night's flash storm. Taking water from this stream was easy, but what they really needed to do was cross over it.

Wise old Gamba marched back and forth at the edge of the muck before deciding, "We'll have to go around it."

"You mean walk an extra mile?" complained one of the twins. "Why don't we just go through it?" "You want to risk drowning or getting stuck?" was Gamba's reply.

Anguka - or Choma - smiled confidently, "I'm sure it's not that deep! Watch, I'll cross it myself. I'll show you."

Despite his father's warning, Anguka/Choma gently set his paws into the mud until they touched solid ground. Before long, he was treading across the drying stream with just small patches of dirt on his fur to show for it. He was halfway across when his pride got to him; "You see, guys? It's easy! I'll be way ahead of you all by--"

Splosh!

The others gasped in surprise as the twin sunk like rock into the deep mud. They waited with baited breath for him to surface. When he did, they all breathed a sigh of relief. However, his father proved to be correct as the teen struggled to swim, gurgling and coughing in panic. "That's it," concluded Zola; "we're taking the long way."

As the others followed in Zola's paw steps, Masada's ears picked up on the rustling of dead grass. Sure enough, the family was being followed. It was Makuu, a distant cousin of the Kivuli clan who had his eyes on a mate for months now. This young and ambitious rover was determined to snag himself a dominant female, and they didn't come more available than Zola.

Masada watched carefully as Makuu's shadow snaked through the grass, biding its time until his quarry was in striking range. As a subordinate, it was not Masada's place to decide Zola's mates for her, but for some unexplainable reason, something about this rover rubbed him the wrong way.

Zola paused to nip at the ants crawling over her tail, when her attention was captured by the voice of a stranger: "Could I be of assistance, m'lady?"

"...Who's that?" she chirped curiously.

The stranger charismatically brushed a curtain of tall grass aside to reveal himself. "My name is Makuu- 'The Ambitious One.'"

Zola's eyes fluttered. "Ambitious?"

"Well of course," he smiled as he inched closer to her; "there are many kinds of ambition, lovely one. The drive for a better home, a bigger meal... a new queen?"

"New queen, eh?" Zola grinned. "So that's what you're after."

Makuu bowed his head at her feet to show submission as he replied, "I'm not the first to come and ask for your approval, am I? Surely a beauty like you gets hounded by rovers every day." Flattered, Zola giggled. "Heh-heh-heh! Oh, no. No, I'm not that attractive."

"But you are," smiled Makuu as he leaned in to stare deeply into her eyes. "I know, because I've traveled many a weary mile in hopes the stars would lead me to my queen. And lo and behold, here you are."

"I think you've got your stars crossed," came Masada from behind the surprised rover; "because this queen here is taken."

"Masada," gasped an equally surprised Zola.

Makuu glared at the young Isibani. "You lie," he said; "I know well enough that you're no king. You're not even tall enough."

Masada slyly replied, "I may not be as big as you, but I can take you on."

"Masada," whispered Zola, "what are you doing?"

"Defending your honor," he whispered back.

Makuu's fur ruffled at the sound of a challenge. "Come on, little pup, let's see how tough you are!"

Standing his ground patiently, Masada turned to his rival and said, "Tell me something, 'Ambitious One,' how brave are you?"

"Braver than you, you meddling worm."

"Are you brave enough to take on a Horus as it's swooping down on you?"

"Are you kidding? I can pluck it out of the sky and rip off all its feathers in just a few seconds. So, come on! Let's go." As he said this, Makuu's tail raised and his legs bounced up and down as if he was war dancing.

Masada gave him a cunning smile. "Alright, alright, we'll have our fight. But I just want you to know that I asked about the Horus for a reason."

"And what reason is that?"

"Because it's coming this way! Horus! Horus!! Take cover, everyone!!"

Masada's warning calls were loud enough to alert the whole clan, and without even thinking twice they headed for cover in the grass.

Makuu, the self-proclaimed Horus killer, screamed in terror and took off in a flash. Masada and Zola watched as the rover unwittingly dashed into the murky river of mud, only to get stuck in it just as Anguka/Choma had earlier. Those who saw this laughed at the fool's mistake as if the stunt was a joke.

Anguka or Choma- whichever fell into the muddy pool- also laughed as he successfully inched out of the stream and grinned at the muddied rover, "Ha! Good luck getting out of that, buddy. Took me about two hours!"

The rest of the clan laughed as they left Makuu, still sinking in the mud. He would get out eventually, but perhaps his pride would never be the same.

The clan settled down in an old abandoned ground squirrel burrow that evening. While the younger family members were reminiscing of better days and grooming each other soothingly, one member of the family seemed most unpleasant. Masada was careful in his approach to his queen. "Uh... Zola? You're not mad at me, are you? About earlier?"

"Huh," she huffed. "I suppose you thought I needed rescuing from that big bad rover, eh?"

"Well I just thought-"

"I just want you to know that I can take care of myself, Masada. I don't need your help," she snapped. This made him hang his head in shame. "I'm sorry."

Seeing as she hurt his feelings a bit, she calmed her nerves. "I know you meant well," she cooed, "but just promise me that next time a rover tries to woo me, let me handle it."

"I promise," nodded Masada.

She then moved away from him and crawled to the edge of the sleeping burrow the family dug up that evening. Before she entered it for a good night's sleep, Zola looked back at Masada with a warm smile. "Thanks for the good laugh, Masada."

He gestured a bow to her in reply; "It was my pleasure, Zola."

The Isibani queen watched as her self-appointed bodyguard walked back to the sleepy pups nearby. A sudden calm fell on her, as if she was relieved to have such a strong, reliable and handsome male nearby.

Then it dawned on her: Did she just think of Masada as handsome? He is the same outsider whom the Great Star Himself cast His disapproving shadow on, isn't he? But just as Zola's old prejudice crept back into her mind, she was quick to remind herself of all the times Masada proved to be a skilled Selket hunter, babysitter, lookout, and now a protective guardian for the queen herself. Much had changed in such a short time, she realized, and on top of all of his good qualities, Masada was also an unrelated and highly available male. All of these thoughts swam in her head just as she was about to retire into her sleeping burrow. Perhaps she was in need of a good night's sleep; she hoped that in the morning her mind would be more at ease...

But a good night's sleep wouldn't come to poor Zola. She tossed and turned in her sandy bed as the voice of her fallen sister Zarina whispered in her dreams:

"Dark clouds cover the horizon. Vultures circle in the air overhead. Dear sister, the time will soon come for you and our family to meet the true lords of the desert. Beware, my sister... Beware the Bastet!"

13

Two days of wandering across open plains with plenty of wind and not enough food had left the Isibani very fatigued. But soon they came to a field with scattered trees that offered them plenty of rest. While the others took a nap under a tree shade, Abeni went forward to act as lookout.

She would return just a few minutes later to wake the family with terrible news: "We're done for! We never should have come this way!"

"What is it, Abeni? What's wrong?" yawned Gamba. "Monsters!" she said in a panic. "Monsters just over the hill! Come and see."

Curiously the family rose from their sandy beds and followed the terrified female to the edge of the dune. Imagine their shock and awe when, for the very first time in their lives, they gazed at the sight of a pride of lions lounging in the next field.

"...By the stars," murmured Gamba. "... Never have I seen such huge creatures."

"They're ...they're bigger than Anubis," gulped one of the twins, Anguka or Choma.

"What are they, Father?" asked the other twin.

Zola slowly and quietly observed the giant cats, particularly the biggest and shaggiest of all. He, the pride's only male, was just as her nightmares described him: mane that stretched from his head and neck like the Great Star's rays. And when he yawned, she could see his fangs, which looked as long and sharp as a Horus' talons.

"No doubt about it," she frowned; "they're hunters all right..."

"We're doomed!" panicked Abeni again.

"Calm yourself!" barked Gamba the patriarch. "We can sneak around them once we find the right path."

"I'll help you out, Gamba," Masada volunteered.

As the veteran and rookie quietly descended the dune, Zola's eyes stayed fixed on the giants in the distance.

"Beware, sister... Beware the Bastet."

Her skin crawled with fear as those haunting words crossed her mind again.

"Zola?" peeped Tamu nearby, "Are you alright?"

Zola blinked herself out of the trance and said, "Yes. I'm fine... Whatever happens, stay together."

"Girls!" called out Masada from the bottom of the dune. "We're ready, let's go." Zola took a gulp and a deep breath before sliding down the hill, along with her equally terrified family.

Gamba and Masada met with the others in a patch of tall grass, which proved to be a perfect blanket for the meerkats as well as their scents. The lazy lions settled in the center of the field were blissfully ignorant of their presence.

"Here's what we're gonna do," whispered the plotting Gamba. "We'll go in groups: Anguka, Choma, you'll go first. Then you, Masada and Abeni. Next will be Imbali and Tamu, and girls, you'll carry with you Ubani and Tundi. Zola and I will carry the other boys, Isibandi and Umoya."

"Which way are we going, Father?" asked Tamu.

Gamba then pointed the way: "There are trees scattered across the field, most of them are to the left. Each group will go as softly and swiftly as they can to each one, and stay there until its safe to move on. At the far end of the field is another dune. My hope is that when we go over it, we'll be out of the hunter's territory."

"It's a brilliant plan, Father," replied Imbali; "... but what should happen if something goes wrong?"

"I thought of that," frowned Gamba. "...One of us who are not carrying a pup will have to distract the hunters while the rest of us escape. In the distance is a fallen tree that will provide a lookout post for that volunteer, and perhaps while inside the hollow log there'll be enough shelter from an attack."

A brief and grim pause fell over the family before Gamba bravely said, "I will do it, as I am the oldest and-"

"No," Masada protested as he stepped forward. "I'll do it."

"What? No!" Zola was quick to disapprove. "I should do it, I'm the High Leader."

"All the more reason why you should stay with the others," argued Masada. "Besides, think of the pups."

Again, Zola shook her head. "I don't like this idea. Those Bastet creatures will tear you apart, Masada."

"...Wait," Masada gave a confused look as he replied. "What is a Bastet?"

Zola pointed toward the distant lions. "Them."

"How do you know what they're called?" asked Masada curiously.

In her frustration, Zola growled, "Oh, what does it matter? You're not going to bait them. I forbid it."

"There's no other way, Zola." Gamba put his foot down. "Masada, make swift to the hollow tree and stay hidden until the Bastet come for us." "Yes, Gamba," Masada nodded, much to Zola's worry.

Gamba noticed the look in her face as she watched her friend scoot away. "Don't worry, my dear. If anyone is best suited for this task, it's Masada." She remained quiet while the others prepared to take flight.

The first ones up were Anguka and Choma. They crouched down in the grass patch until King Bastet rolled on his side to take a nap. Then the twins scuttled across the field like beetles, until they made it to the first tree. In their triumph, they bopped heads. They would then proceed to the next safe haven, and the next, until they made it to the dune with hardly any stir from the Bastet King or his three mates.

Next up were Abeni, Imbali, and Tamu. Each carried a pup in their mouth to ensure their safety. Like the twins, they patiently waited for the lions to lay still and look away, then they took off for the tree as fast as the wind. One of the lionesses opened a curious eye, but missed potential prey as it hid behind a tree. She then yawned and went back to sleep.

Finally, it was time for Gamba and Zola, with young Tundi in her mouth. The pup trembled with fear, "I'm scared, Zola." "Hush child." Grampa Gamba was quick to say. "Remember: no peeps, not a single one until we make it to the red dune." The pup nodded, but her eyes still glimmered with fear.

The lions remained in their sleep, allowing Gamba to lead his small group toward the first tree. They made it there with no incident, but Zola couldn't help but peer around the tree trunk to see where Masada was. Sure enough, he could be seen halfway up the dead trunk. He stared intently at the lions, ready to face them head on if they were to awaken.

"Zola," whispered Gamba, "move now."

Zola scooped up Tundi and away they galloped toward tree number two, which was five feet away. When they got there, they paused to breathe. Zola let go of little Tundi to relax herself, when she heard an unsettling cry in the sky.

"Horus!" squealed Tundi, before hiding behind Gamba.

The elder meerkat was quick to scout the sky and whispered, "Not Horus. Vultures."

Zola was quickly overcome with horror, as her late sister Zarina's voice filled her mind once again:

"Dark clouds on the horizon... Vultures circle overhead..."

Zola started to tremble visibly, which grabbed the attention of Gamba and Tundi. "Zola! What's wrong?" asked her father. "...Zola, speak to me."

"It's the end," she whispered while in her trance. "... We're all doomed. Vultures mean death. We're doomed!"

Gamba was quick to approach her and hip-slam her into consciousness. "Zola," he barked, "get a hold of yourself! What's gotten into you?"

Her eyes met with his as she trembled in reply, "Father... I saw the Bastet in my dreams. I should have told you sooner, but it's true. These are the monsters that came to Zarina in her dream."

"Zarina?"

"Yes, don't you remember her vision? And she's come to me now, in my dreams. It's all true... I should have listened to her..."

Gamba held onto Tundi, whom was trembling herself now thanks to Zola's outburst. "Child," he murmured to Zola, "please calm yourself. The vultures are not our enemies, in fact, they may lead the Bastet away from us, and that's a good thing!"

Zola rested her tearful face on her father's strong chest and started sobbing. "She was a far greater leader than I ever gave her credit for... I never should have challenged her."

"Shh, shh..." cooed Gamba as he nuzzled her in comfort. "It's alright, Zola. Everything will be alright as long as we keep our heads and stick together."

The matriarch then took a deep sigh before lifting her head. "You're right, father. We still have to get to that dune."

"Bark! Bark! Bark! Bark! Bark!"

Zola gasped in surprise. "That's Masada's bark!" She removed herself from the safety of the tree to discover Masada's fate.

Just as Gamba had predicted, the crying vultures had awakened the lion pride. Fearful that they might pick up the scent of his family, Masada had perched himself atop the hollow tree stump and started to bark like crazy at them. Now their attention was redirected to him, and they prepared themselves to stalk him.

"No," Zola gasped softly, but her father commanded, "Now's our chance. Let's fly to the dune, now!" With that, he snatched up little Tundi and galloped off. With hardly any other choice, Zola reluctantly followed after her father.

Masada courageously challenged the curious lions by dancing around the fallen tree as if to taunt them. It was doing the trick; the male lion in particular was licking his lips as he approached the energetic meerkat. With their stomachs rumbling, the three lionesses quickened their pace from a stalk, to a trot, to a full gallop. With nowhere to run, Masada jumped inside the hollow stump. There, he was a sitting target.

The lions surrounded the half tree to make sure their prey couldn't escape. One by one, they clawed the dry bark until its outer skin cracked. From inside the tree, Masada could hear the cracking of wood, the panting of the lions, and within moments, the whole floor of his hiding place started to rumble. He gulped, knowing his hunters were now using their full force on the stump, trying to push it out from under its roots.

To Masada's amazement, the Bastet King ripped a large part of the tree stump's top with his fangs. The young meerkat could now see the beast's nose and lips dipping into the entrance, intent on snatching Masada by any means necessary. Closer and closer the beast's muzzle came to him, cornering him as his hiding place became more torn and shaken. Surely this was the end for the brave meerkat; he believed it to be so while a strange calm had come over him. He closed his eyes to welcome death... But death would not answer.

The Bastet King's muzzle pulled back suddenly, and the aggravated beast let out a painful roar. Something had bitten his foot while he was caught off guard, and that something was none other than Zola.

Alarmed, the lionesses stopped their assault on the tree stump and focused on their king. He shook his leg, indicating that the bite was enough to startle if not harm him. That's when Zola made her bold move to the shredded tree stump.

"Masada!" she barked frantically. "Masada, it's me!"

"Zola?!" he gasped as he popped his head out.

"Hurry, run!" she commanded, while eyeing the deterred lions.

Masada scrambled out of the stump just in time, and together he and Zola galloped at top speed toward a large patch of brown grass, where the lions were once lying about. They dove into the grass just as the lions lunged themselves at them.

The two meerkats were out of breath, but now that they were in a new hiding place, they knew that panting would be their downfall. Both Zola and Masada held their breath as they slinked further into the grass. The lions, having no color vision, could only sniff out their prey in such a mesh. And it was fortunate for the meerkats that the lions' own fresh scene was all over the place. Luck seemed to be on their side, but Masada and Zola knew they were hardly out of danger.

The meerkat pair huddled together in the center of the patch, wisely choosing to lay low and not move while the Bastet clan moved in. From where they laid, Zola and Masada could see the shadows of the giant predators circling them and inching ever closer to them. Zola began to tremble, but sympathetic Masada moved closer to her until his hip was locked only for a moment. It wasn't long before one of the lions was standing right over them. Even then, as death seemed to be staring them straight in the face, the meerkats neither budged nor made a sound. This would prove to be their saving grace.

Low roars came from over the red dune in the direction the Isibani clan had gone. The lions all lifted their heads in response to the calls. Two young lionesses came bounding with joy toward the rest of the pride, beckoning them to come forward. As if completely forgetting the hidden meerkats, the whole pride took flight toward and over the dune.

Both Masada and Zola breathed a deep sigh of relief, but their joy soon turned to panic. "My stars," gasped Zola, "they're heading straight for the family!"

The meerkat pair couldn't catch up with the Bastet clan, nor did they wish to. They could only hope and pray that their relatives were safely hiding somewhere over the dune.

They stopped at the very top of the red dune to oversee their enemies headed east, toward the corpse of a slaughtered antelope which the young lionesses were dragging homeward. Both Masada and Zola were now free to breathe easily; the enemy was now preoccupied with something other than meerkat meat, and that meant that not only were they safe, but so was the rest of their clan. And as it turned out, the Isibani were not far away.

"Masada! Zola! Over here," called out one of the twins from the base of the red dune.

Standing high on their hind legs by a large rock formation was the rest of the clan. The sight of them brought tears of joy to Zola's eyes as she and Masada skid down the slope to reunite with them.

As the younger ones nuzzled the returning pair, Gamba raised his head toward the lions in the distance. "Come, let's get moving while they're preoccupied."

"Won't they follow us?" asked young Tundi nervously.

Her grandfather nudged her to move forward as he replied, "You needn't worry about them anymore, dear. We're hardly a morsel compared to that meal."

And with that, the meerkats quietly left the Bastet clan to devour their meal and swat at the swooping vultures.

Dusk came all too quickly for the weary Isibani; though they needed sleep, what they needed more was food. But no one complained about their hunger when they discovered an abandoned burrow with freshly-dug up holes. This was a prime spot to spend the night; however, Gamba was the first to suspect trouble.

The veteran leader sniffed around and inside the main tunnel and concluded, "The Kivuli have been here... They must be a day ahead of us, but it's clear we're headed in their direction."

The family exchanged looks of fret; half-starved, they were by no means prepared for any confrontation. Then

Zola spoke up, "We'll worry about that when the time comes. Let's just try to sleep for now."

In agreement, most of the family began to crawl into the burrow without uttering a word.

Zola was about to bed down herself when her she heard Masada's soft voice: "Zola? Can I talk to you for a second?"

Though tired, Zola was obliged to approach her young friend, "Yes, what is it Masada?"

"I just want to thank you for saving my life today..."

"Oh, it was nothing."

"Well you really didn't have to. I mean, you shouldn't have; you could've been killed."

"Masada, you're my responsibility, as are all my family members."

"... Family?" he mused. "I thought I was just a no-account outsider."

Zola's eyes beamed, "I didn't mean it when I said that!"

"Well," the young male frowned and bowed his head, "we were never really good friends anyway."

"Masada," replied the young queen in a surprisingly gentle voice, "much has changed over time... I've changed. I only acted tough around you because I was afraid of you."

"You? Afraid of me?" he smirked in surprise.

"Yes," confessed Zola. "You were a stranger, I just didn't know what to expect from you. But now I see you for who you are, and..." She turned away as she paused.

"...And?" persisted the curious male.

Trying not to show here flushed cheeks, Zola tilted her head toward him to say, "I guess what I'm trying to say is... I like you."

Masada moved in closer until the two of them were face to face. He smiled at her in a way that seemed to speak volumes. "I like you too."

As their dark eyes locked, a silent and mysterious force came over them; their heartbeats quickened, and their paws were itching to touch. It seemed that nothing could break this silent vibe between them... except Gamba. "Ahem," coughed the patriarch nearby.

"Huh? Oh..." the two meerkats broke their mental lock and turned away in shyness.

"It's getting late you two," spoke Gamba in a deep, stern tone. "Let's be off to bed then."

"Right," sighed Zola. "Goodnight Father, Masada."

Knowing now that her father was watching closely, the young matriarch crawled into the burrow without daring to look back. Masada was quick to follow her, but he stopped in his tracks when he heard Gamba say, "Masada. Come here for a minute."

With a twinge of fear, the young male approached his superior.

Gamba sat up on his hind legs as he spoke in his usual fatherly tone; "Zola is our High Leader and needs a king worthy of her, but in my eyes she is first and foremost my daughter."

"Yes, sir." Masada humbly bowed before Gamba.

"I want what's best for her."

"Sir," replied the young male almost fearfully, "I would never challenge your authority."

"Hm," smirked the elder meerkat. "Someday soon, you won't have to."

Masada froze in his place as Gamba slowly walked over to the burrow. It was just the two of them now, veteran and rookie. Gamba was now more comfortable then ever to reveal his true intentions:

"I have led this family for over six years. Now here I am, over ten years old... You know, not many of us reach such an age. But anyway, I am no longer fit to lead this family."

"Gamba, don't say that."

"But it's true," replied Gamba somberly. "My daughter is now a queen, and a queen needs a mate that can provide pups for her. The truth is, Masada, my reign ended with the death of my beloved Isibani."

Masada showed his sympathy by bowing his head.

Gamba went on to say, "I will stay with you all until we have settled in a new home, where I'll know for certain my young ones will be safe and sound. When that day comes, I will move on."

"No," shook Masada's head. "You can't leave us, Gamba. We need you now more than ever, even if we ever do settle down somewhere, how will we cope without our King?"

The elder meerkat gave him a gentle smile. "My friend, a new king has already been chosen." Then without saying another word, Gamba headed underground for the night.

Masada remained outside until the sun completely disappeared on the horizon. But even then, he was troubled. Was Gamba right, he wondered? Was he going to be the new king of the clan? The more he wondered about it, the more uncertain Masada felt about his worthiness.

14

Every journey, no matter how long or how treacherous, eventually comes to an end. For the Kivuli clan, the end of their tiring trek across the desert was heralded by a sudden thunderstorm that swept across the plains overnight.

When Shujaa, proud leader of the clan, opened his eyes the next morning, it sounded as if the thunder stayed behind. The whole family was stirred out of their sleep by soft "booms" and quaking sand within the burrow. The smallest members whimpered in fear, thinking the Great Star was angry with them for reasons unknown. Shujaa had no fear of thunder, but that wasn't the only reason why he exited the burrow to explore. At his age, he knew that there was more to this strange thumping sound than there seemed. When he gazed out into the open, his suspicions were confirmed, much to his delight.

"Come out, children!" he called into the burrow. "Come out and see them."

One by one, five young pups peeked out from the safety of the burrow, and gazed in wide-eyed wonder at an awesome sight: elephants on the march.

"Daddy, what are they?" chirped the female.

"Thunder-walkers," smiled Shujaa. "They are the moving mountains of the earth. They come all the way from the land beyond the desert in search for water. If we keep a safe distance from them, they may lead us to it."

The pups were quick to pester their mother Busara as soon as she exited the burrow. "Come on, Mom!" they barked, "we wanna follow the thunder-walkers!"

Busara yawned sleepily before giving Shujaa an ugly look in her eyes. "You just had to get them started, didn't you?"

"It'll be good for them," insisted her mate. "Where there's water there's good pickings of Selket to be had."

"Fine, dear... but first we warm up." Busara sat up and leaned into the morning sunlight.

The whole family soon joined her in sunbathing; they were nearly twice in numbers now then they were since Masada was proclaimed dead over two years earlier. Some of his siblings had already moved on, but Jasiri remained a loyal soldier of his father's growing army.

Tani, the most vital of all babysitters, also remained with the Kivuli. She was coming close to the age of becoming a queen herself, and had already been the target for many a rover's affections. But Tani was a patient meerkat; she knew her day would come, but not for a while longer. She still had much to learn, and she knew it.

Now at a mature age, Naima was also a shining example of her mother's leadership. She could now care for her younger siblings as well Tani, and would even volunteer for such an energy-sapping task. Perhaps deep down, she was still missing her twin brother Masada, whose true fate was known only to her. The pups were always there to distract her, which would explain her willingness to nurture them constantly. She was the first to tire of sun-bathing.

"I'm ready," declared Naima. "Let's go now."

"Yay!" cheered the enthusiastic pups, as they burst into a charge. "Thunder-walk with us, Naima!"

"Keep a safe distance, children!" warned Shujaa as he followed after them. "I've known one foolish meerkat who ended up on the wrong end of a thunder-walker's foot!"

"Boom! Boom! Crash!" went the pups, who were now playfully imitating the rumble of an elephant's stomping foot. How they wished that they could move the earth the way those grey giants could.

As enjoyable as it was to follow in the footsteps of the mighty behemoths, the family had to step aside when the small elephant herd came to a halt at a small river, made exclusively of rain water. For the pups, watching the elephants slurp up gallons of water with noses that looked like Wadjets attached to their faces was all the entertainment they needed. But the adults were now focused on searching for grubs and bugs. As Shujaa had predicted, bugs by the dozens flocked to the soft soil like bees to honey. A meerkat banquet was brewing.

Naima led the five pups to their first pantry of solid food. She and her yearling brother would catch and chew the yummy worms, then split the fragments between the boisterous pups. The older family members were quick to lap up what puddle water there was left while the elephants started to march off into the air-rippling heat toward the horizon.

The only one not eating or playing was old Shujaa, standing guard atop a hill and surveying the land. He knew better than anyone that trouble could jump out at any given time and from any corner. But after standing guard for almost an hour, even he was beginning to fall under the calming spell of the warm sunlight. But his vigilance was about to pay off. His head started to hang low while dozing off, when his sharp nose caught an unfamiliar scent. Immediately, the old general stood straight up in alert. His eyes scanned the tall golden grass that covered the hill he stood atop of, in search of impending doom. Sure enough, the figure of a small animal was creeping in the grass, as if using it as a cover.

"Kivuli! Kivuli, to me!" shouted Shujaa. "It's an alert! Alert, my children!"

Meanwhile, Masada was beginning to think his luck was changing for the better. He and his down-trodden family were following the fresh smell of flowers and water, and now here he was just several feet away from the waterhole. All he and his friends had to do now was cross over the large hill of grass that stood in their way. But then, suddenly, meerkat barks rung out in the air - and worse yet - they were coming from someone whose voice was unrecognizable. He jumped to his hind quarters and barked, "Isibani! Isibani, alert! Strangers are here!"

Nearby, Zola and the others heard the call and ran to his side.

Likewise, the Kivuli clan joined Shujaa on the top of the hill, looking down on the gathering army below.

The grass between the two families was so thick, neither one could tell each others' numbers. This would bode well for the outnumbered Isibani, but they were by no means prepared for a fight. Zola was all set to lead a retreat, when she noticed how still Masada was. He stood there like a statue, staring glossy-eyed at the enemies ahead. She could tell that something was troubling him, more so than any recent threats.

"Masada?" she purred as she joined his side.

Neither Masada nor Zola were prepared to hear his reply. "It's them... It's my family."

It took her only a few seconds to realize what he meant, but still felt a little uncertain if his eyes weren't playing tricks on him. "Are you sure?"

"It's them," he nodded slowly. "It's definitely them."

Zola noticed that his forearms were starting to tremble, a sign of his anxiety. "We'll go before they can charge. We'll even lower our tails to show them we're just passing by."

When faced with any other clan, Masada may have agreed with his queen's decision. But the Kivuli was anything but just another clan.

"No," he murmured. "I have to face them."

"No you don't," Zola shook her head worriedly. "Let's just go before they think we're in war mode."

He then turned to look her in the eye, never before so sternly. "Zola, I have to do this. You take the family and get them to a safe distance. I'll see if I can talk to them.

"Masada," frowned Zola, "as long as I've known, no one has ever talked an enemy clan out of battle..."

He remained silent, still gazing into her eyes as if his very soul was debating with hers. Finally, she sighed in concession.

"Alright, you do what you have to. Just don't get yourself killed, you hear me?"

"Understood." His head then turned back to the Kivuli.

Zola signaled to her family to slowly turn tail and leave. They quietly followed her lead, but not without looking back at the one steadfast soldier who chose to stay behind.

"Look," said Busara as she watched the mysterious intruders turn in their direction. "They're retreating. Thank the stars."

Shujaa, who stood by her side, had his eyes on another figure who was shifting through the grass. "Wait, Busara... One of them is coming closer. I better go down there and investigate."

"I'll go with you."

"Me too," announced Jasiri nearby. Before his parents could argue, the scarred warrior led the charge.

"Stay here," said Shujaa to his remaining children. He followed quickly after Jasiri, sure that he could deal with the stranger with nothing more than a brief warning- followed by a swift sharp bite.

The meerkats met in the middle, their families at a safe distance anxiously awaiting their fate. Shujaa and Jasiri both towered over the young male, who was obviously out of his league. He didn't even have the luxury of long sharp fangs dripping from his mouth like they did. Their distrust in him quickly transformed into curiosity.

Then suddenly, he spoke. "I speak on behalf of the others when I say we mean you no harm."

"We don't need your negotiation," hissed Jasiri, "We just need you to leave."

"Jasiri, let me handle this," said Shujaa as he brushed his son aside. "I see your family is already leaving, stranger. You'd be wise to follow them."

"I would," replied Masada, "except that I have two families: those who gave me life, and those who've raised me."

Shujaa raised an eyebrow. "Are you telling me you're leaving one clan for another?"

"I'm telling you what I have known to be the truth... Father."

Shujaa and Jasiri both gasped in wonder, while their rival added, "I am your son Masada, brother of Naima and Kivuli. My brother and I were chased by an Anubis. But I survived and was taken in by the Isibani clan. They're good people, and I can assure you that we would never take what's rightfully yours – your land, your food, your right to survive. All we ask for is a safe passage to the land beyond your borders. Let us settle there, and I can promise you we will never be a bother to your clan again."

Shujaa paused to take it all in. At first, the young male's words were ridiculous nonsense, but the more he listened, the more awestruck he became. He clearly recalled finding Anubis tracks on the day the Great Star fell into shadow. He remembered his grown daughter Naima rambling about seeing her long-lost brother. But most prominent of all came a memory he dared to recover from the darkest corners of his mine, a memory he believed to have forgotten about until now...

> *Shujaa inched closer to the cornered pups, ready to tear each one apart, when suddenly one of them sat up in defiance and cried out, "Dad, it's me! It's Masada! Don't you recognize me?"*
> *"Do you think me a fool, little worm?"*
> *"W-worm? ...D-dad, it's me! It's me!!"*

That voice came back to Shujaa like a slap in the face. He stepped back and faltered, as if he had seen a ghost. And there was the ghost, all grown up, staring back at him. But even in this moment of epiphany, the proud old general could not bring himself to the truth.

"No... it can't be."

"I was the 'worm,' Father."

"You LIE!" roared Shujaa. "My son Masada died along with his brother in the wilderness. You're a spy, a trickster!"

"You dare play with our leader's feelings?" hissed Jasiri to Masada. "I ought to rip you to shreds where you stand!"

"Don't you dare!" shouted the voice of Busara.

The boys were then forced to move aside for the queen of the Kivuli, who had overheard everything from a nearby standpoint. No longer able to keep to herself, she crept up to her estranged son until they were nose to nose.

"...Masada?"

"Yes, mom. It's me," he nodded.

Just as she once promised Naima, this truly was the brightest day in Busara's life. Where her mate saw a trickster, she saw her lost son reborn. "Bless my stars," she murmured as she joyfully nuzzled Masada's face. "My son... My baby. You're alive!"

"Busara," chirped a disapproving Shujaa, but his mate ignored him.

"Naima told me you were alive," said Busara to Masada, "but I had to see it for myself." She then raised her head toward the sun and proclaimed something she hadn't in a long time, "Praise Nyota-Kuu!"

"Busara!" growled Shujaa. "Don't fall for that imposter's lies."

The Kivuli queen inched Masada closer to his Father. "It's him, Shujaa. Look at him! Look at his eyes. How could you not see your likeness in him?"

The old king stepped forward, maintaining his disbelief yet restraining from acting on aggression. "If you are my son, then why do you side with the enemy?"

Masada calmly replied, "Because they've spared my life when it would have been easier just to take it. I've learned from them, Father; I've learned that we all just want what's best for our young. You fight for yours, and they fight for theirs. In a way, we're all alike. If only we could find a way to share the land."

"Share the land?! Ridiculous," barked Shujaa. "In all my long years as ruler, I have never seen such a thing as two families sharing their resources. We take what we can because if we didn't, we would starve!"

"There has to be another way."

"There IS no other way! Now... you have a choice to make. You can rejoin our family and we can leave all that's come between us in the past, or you can go back and help your friends. But I must warn you, Masada: if you choose them over us, then I will be forced to denounce you as my son."

The young male, whose wisdom and selflessness touched his mother's heart, was now at a crossroads. It delighted him to no end to hear his father call him by his real name, and to once again be nuzzled and embraced by his mother. And yet, not even those reasons could pull him away from Zola, who was growing ever more closely to him. And more still, his foster family was still without a home, lost in an unfriendly wilderness. His responsibility – his duty – was with them.

He looked back at his mother with sad eyes; "Mom... I'm so sorry. I wish you could understand."

She nodded with a heavy heart. "I do understand, my son. They need you..."

He then took one last glance at his disappointed father and his bewildered brother Jasiri. "Goodbye." He turned around and galloped back into the dense grass toward the trail of the Isibani.

It all could have ended right then and there, with bittersweet goodbyes; if only Jasiri were as complacent with Masada's departure as his parents were. So here he was, the long-lost son of the Kivuli, turning his back on them to rejoin his kidnappers. No, it was not something Jasiri could sit back and accept. This was insulting... This was treason!

"Traitor," he hissed underneath his breath as he poised to strike. Before his parents could stop him, Jasiri bolted after Masada with teeth ready to chomp down on him. When they collided, both families from opposite sides of the hill could see it.

"Masada is under attack!" cried out Zola in horror. She then lined up her family in an attacking formation. "Charge!" Like a wildfire they raced through the grass.

"A war dance," gulped Naima, who saw this to her horror. "They're coming. It's an ambush!"

"Stay here with the pups," said Tani. "We'll aid Mother and Father. Brothers, sisters, attack!" Like lava off an erupting volcano, they charged down the hill.

The two forces met in the center, where chaos awaited them. From all sides, yelps and growls rang out. Fangs gnashed, claws sheered, fur flew.

Amidst it all was Masada, furiously fighting off the vengeful Jasiri. As the older male bit down hard on his little brother's tail, Masada clawed at Jasiri's face defensively.

"Oh no, you don't," hissed Jasiri as he recalled the scarring Masada gave him before. "Not this time!"

He was about to give Masada a bite to the face, when Zola blindsided him and pushed him off Masada.

Both Shujaa and Busara were also rushed by on-coming Isibani, but they were better prepared than their impulsive son. They each had two enemies to contain with at once, before the rest of the Kivuli clan rushed to their rescue.

The younger Isibani members – Umoya, Ubani and Tundi – stood at the edge of the grasses for safety, but from their perspective they couldn't see which family was winning and which was losing.

"Stop!" cried out Zola in the middle of the melee. "Isibani, we're outnumbered! Retreat to the river!"

"Retreat! Retreat!" echoed other meerkats as the Kivuli gained the upper hand.

But one Kivuli member, Busara, took pity on the rival clan while her subordinates continued to assault them. "Pull back, everyone! Pull back," she loudly commanded, but no one seemed to hear her as they chased off the retreating Isibani. Finally, she caught up to her mate Shujaa, whose jaws had entrapped Gamba's lower leg. She tugged at his ear furiously. "Shujaa, enough! Stop this-"

"RAWR!" he let out, turning around quickly. In that one brief moment, he mistook her for an enemy, and slammed his fangs onto her nose. Busara yelped and slapped at Shujaa's snout. With that, the Kivuli fell still and silent. All eyes were now on the stunned king and queen.

Realizing his error, Shujaa humbly frowned, "Busara... D-dearest. I didn't – I thought you were... Forgive me."

Busara stood tall among her subordinates, her dark eyes glaring with fury, staring intently on Shujaa and Jasiri. "I am ashamed of you. All of you! Our Masada had come back to us after years of separation, and you've chased him away!"

"He's made his choice," replied Shujaa while defending Jasiri's actions, "and we have our laws to uphold."

"Laws, rules, restrictions. What good are they if they leave our family scattered and broken?" Busara protested. "I believe it's time for a new set of rules, children; rules that do not turn us into war-mongering..." Her voice faded to a whisper, then she stopped speaking altogether. "...Do you hear that?" murmured the queen to her king.

Shujaa's ears perked up as he quickly scanned the area. "... Is that a pup calling?"

Initially, Busara believed the cries to be that of her own pups. "Dear heavens, the pups! They must have gotten lost in the grass. Hurry, everyone! Find them!"

Naima was called to assist in the frantic search, and by high noon, all five of Busara's pups were rounded up and secured... and yet, a pup's cries remained in the air.

The family continued to search until Naima picked up the scent of the Isibani clan. It led her straight to a most unexpected find: a lone female pup, unrelated to the family and shivering fearfully in a curled up ball. Young Tundi watched and waited as the enemy clan soon surrounded her.

Nature is a fickle mistress. She blesses a family with pups one day, and then takes them away the next. She provides the snake with the pups and provides the eagle with the snake. Her seasons are either too hot and dry, or too cold and muggy. And just when one believes that he's got her weather patterns figured out, she hits him with a sandstorm. She is no one's friend, and no one's enemy. But on the day he lost Tundi, Masada couldn't help but think that Mother Nature had it out for him. He trailed the downtrodden Isibani clan on their resumed trek for a new home, with a hung head.

The whole family was heartbroken and felt guilty about picking a fight they had no chance in winning. But what was done was done; they were defeated, they had lost Tundi, and they had no choice but to move on. The rest of the family decided to wait until they found a safe place to rest before mourning their loss. Tragedy was no stranger to these resilient meerkats: but for Masada, who had lost more than a niece that afternoon (more like a whole family), the guilt was almost too much to bear. For him, it was as if he were reliving the day he lost his brother Kivuli to an Anubis while the Great Star slept in darkness. And the more he thought about it, the slower he walked.

Zola caught him looking back at the path back to the elephant drinking pools, and sighed in realization of his distress. She trotted from the front of the marching party to the back where Masada greeted her with a gentle nuzzle.

"I have to go back," he whispered.

"Masada... Tundi is gone. They would never take pity on an enemy pup – that's just their way."

"Your sister took pity on me."

"That was different," she insisted. "You were all alone; Tundi was in the middle of a battlefield."

Masada closed his weary eyes and sighed. "...There may still be time to save her. Let me go back and search."

"No. It's too dangerous. Please, Masada... the clan needs you... I need you."

The young male couldn't help but smile in reaction to his queen's affectionate tone of voice. But again he argued, "Give me this one chance, Zola. All of this is my fault-"

"No, it isn't."

"It is. I should have known a fight would break out. I need to try this, for Tundi's sake. I can't stand the thought that my family..."

Masada stopped with a certain look of guilt in his eyes, as if he was ashamed to call the Kivuli clan his "family." "That... that the Kivuli clan... might have killed Tundi because of me."

Zola's heart melted – partly because she pitied him, and partly because she was flattered with his sincere concern for her little niece. "Masada," cooed Zola, "I can't imagine how torn your heart is... You should probably see them anyway – alone this time, so that there's no false attacks this time."

He nodded his thanks to her before making a quick turn back on the beaten path.

"Masada... please be careful."

He looked upon Zola once more before galloping off toward the elephant drinking pools.

"Shadow of the Star," he called himself sometimes. He had chased the Great Star back when he was a pup, on an impossible quest to find its sleeping burrow. Now, on the evening of his final quest, Masada was running in the direction of the setting sun. He knew that once his sun god slipped into the earth on the horizon, time would run out for Tundi – and for him as well.

He had been told as a pup that he was the reason why the Great Star turned black, and that he was cursed. As an adult, he was never really sure if what happened to Kivuli – to Ushomi – to Zarina – or to Tundi – were all coincidence, or if it was all because of him. None of that should have mattered as he ran like the wind into his former clan's territory, but he couldn't help but think back on all of those dark days. Was Imbasa-Kulu punishing him? Or was it Nyota-Kuu? Was it all because of his indecision between which names to call his god? Did any of it matter?

Masada's heart skipped a beat once the scent of the Kivuli clan collided with his nose. He found himself back on the battlefield, which was now reduced to a quiet hill, its grasses dancing in the wind. The scent was still strong though, and Masada followed it like a bloodhound into uncharted territory. They headed Far East, into open dust fields. The sky was already turning from deep blue to black.

Hanging in the sky like a beacon was the moon – "Mother Mweza" as Zola called her. Masada looked up at her with admiration; perhaps she could add some light to the evening, was his hope. He pointed his nose to the dusty earth and tread on. At some point during this frantic search, he found himself praying:

"Please... Great Star, Great Moon, all stars. Please, hear me. I don't know what your real names are, if you're alive or not, or even if you can hear me. But I am in desperate need of your help. I've lost my little sister, you see... I don't know if I'm too late to save her or not, but I have to try finding her... I know I'm not worthy or your service, great ones; I've been foolish and selfish at times. I've put many a loved one in danger, and I know that no amount of grieving or praying will undo my losses. All I ask is this one chance. Just one chance, to put mistakes behind me. I ask you... No, I beg you... Please help me."

His prayers would go unanswered, but that didn't stop Masada from searching for Tundi. His heart told him that she was still alive, waiting to be found. There was still the possibility that she had escaped the wrath of the Kivuli. That small hope was enough to keep him going.

In spite of the flurry of dust surrounding the plain, Masada's nose pin-pointed his former family's scent all the way to its source. There, in the heart of the barren field, sat a well carved-out burrow that would have been perfect for either a ground squirrel colony or a meerkat clan. It was either by chance of fate that this burrow was home to the latter.

Masada softened his step as he approached the burrow entrance, knowing that he could be seen as an intruder and therefore open to an attack. He gulped before dipping his head into the mouth of the burrow, hoping to sniff out any signs of life.

At that point, his heart rate was quickened in a rush of panic; maybe this wasn't such a good idea. Maybe it was too late to save Tundi. Why would they, the enemy, bring her back here alive? That wasn't part of meerkat culture, taking in rival pups. It just didn't make any sense. But then he told himself, the Isibani took him in. Maybe deep down, the Kivuli would do the same. Maybe they weren't so cold and ruthless toward the young... No. No, he knew his father too well. He would never allow himself to...

His thoughts stopped and his heart sank. Then Masada found himself staring into the abyss of an enemy burrow. His time had run out. "Oh, Tundi... I'm so sorry."

The last golden rays of the sun touched the earth as Masada slowly crept away from the enemy burrow. He could see his shadow trail farther across the land than ever before. It was a humbling moment, being one with the earth and sun. Perhaps, in a strange way, he truly was the Great Star's shadow. He mused to himself in a hum as he turned away from the burrow.

"Masada?"

Taken by surprise, he jumped in a gasp and whipped himself around. There before him appeared his twin sister, Naima. It would seem that she heard him, or at least smelled him, upon arrival.

At first, he didn't know what to say, so he sputtered, "I... uh... I just came to... uh... I--"

"You lost your little girl this afternoon."

He bit his lip, sensing that his worst fears had come true. They did find Tundi. He was too late.

"... I knew you'd come looking for her," his sister smiled, just as he began to hang his head in shame.

Curious by his sister's tone of voice, he watched as she slipped back into the burrow without saying another word.

Imagine his surprise when he saw here reemerge, this time carrying a precious young pup in her mouth.

"Tundi??"

"Masada!" squealed the joyful pup.

Naima released the young female so that she could run into the arms of her foster brother. They cuddled and cooed, while Naima looked on proudly.

"As soon as I saw her, I had to do something. I wouldn't let anyone else touch her, because I knew... I hoped you would come back."

"Sister," replied Masada. "I can't thank you enough for this..."

Naima nodded. "I don't want there to be any more trouble between our clans. Wherever you go, we won't follow. Whatever you eat, we won't steal. That's my solemn vow, brother."

Masada gave her a soft nuzzle on her face, as both a thanks and a last goodbye. "Thank you. I'll never forget this."

Masada gently scooped up little Tundi by the nape of her neck and began to trot away. He only paused to look back once, and when he did, he saw not one but three meerkats looking back. It was Naima, her mother Busara, and her father Shujaa. Neither one made an attempt to follow him, just to see him off. He gave them a nod of thanks, and they nodded back. That would be the last time they ever saw their long-lost Masada again, but their memory of him would not soon be forgotten.

15.

It was during the height of summer, when the wind sent flower seeds dancing across the green meadows, which Gamba had decided to leave the Isibani clan. On that morning, he gave his children loving cuddles and words of wisdom that they could live by. None of them felt prepared for this moment, but that could be said about any family on the verge of change.

His last company was with Masada and Zola, the new leaders of the clan. To them he said, "This family is yours now – you are the Zola clan. I trust my children and theirs in your care."

"Yes, Father," bowed his daughter humbly.

Gamba gave Masada a nudge. "You take care of her, too."

"Of course I will," smiled Masada.

"I may see you all again someday, but if not, know that my star will shine brightly in the sky for you."

The former king then said his last goodbyes before moving off. Such was the way for all seasoned meerkats – love, loss, and starting over. In his heart, Masada knew that his time to move on would come. But at least for now, he was with Zola – his mate, and his love.

The Zola clan was off to a good start.

"Sit down my dears," smiled Busara to her newest litter of pups during that same summer, "and I will tell you a story:

"Not so long ago, our family was blessed with a pup named Masada. He was kind, he was brave, and he was very wise. But the winds were envious, and wanted him all to themselves. So one day, when we least expected, the winds carried Masada away. All the land mourned our loss, and even Nyota-Kuu cried. But just when we had lost all hope, our Masada was found again. He had been traveling many a mile to return to us, but it wasn't long before the winds picked him back up and carried him away again.

"The point of this story, my dears, is that Masada is still out there, living his life in lands unknown. And so, we must all be cautious of our neighbors, leave them to their lands and care not for their food. Let them live as they let us live... For never forget that one of them is your brother."

Dedications

To the Kalahari Meerkat Project,*
Animal Planet*
And the makers of "Meerkat Manor,"*
Whose combined efforts to document the lives of real
meerkats have inspired this story.
*All rights reserved.

To my friend and personal transcriber,
Emilie McDonald.

And to my family,
Who have waited so long to read my work.

Love you guys.

-Kristin Downs